I Rode With Cullen Baker

FOREWORD

Cullen Baker was a real person. He lived and died in the Sulphur River country of East Texas.

The only source used in this novel was *Cullen Baker: Premier Gunfighter* by Ed Bartholomew, which gave me the name of the outlaw I had seen in the shadowy firelight when he and Jessica met. Orr's account is reprinted in this cornerstone source, and proved that Cully's whereabouts during the time he was with "Jess" were unaccounted for.

In 2001 the screenplay adaptation of this novel won the Split-Screenplay $1000 competition.

Other sources can now be found by searching online for Cullen Baker. Among these are *The First Fast Draw*, a novel by Louis L'Amour; "Cullen Baker: Purveyor of Death," an article by Al Eason in the September 1966 issue of *Frontier Times*; and *Cullen Montgomery Baker, Reconstruction Desperado*, an extensive and inclusive work by Barry A. Crouch and Donaly E. Brice (LSU Press, 1997).

Of special note is Robert T. Russell, to whom I owe a debt of gratitude for the use of his photograph of the Sulphur River that appears slightly altered as the front cover of this book.

With his father, Traylor Russell, he wrote *Some Die Twice* (Texian Press, 1979), which is available on the secondary market, and likely through interlibrary loan. His death in 2010 ended a correspondence and friendship that cannot be replaced, but left memories of a caring, erudite, and treasured individual.

I Rode With Cullen Baker
A Tale of Romance and Adventure

by
RLB Hartmann

Catawba River Press
Morganton, North Carolina

I Rode with Cullen Baker

A Tale of Romance and Adventure

Second Edition
© 2013 by RLB Hartmann
All Rights Reserved

ISBN-13: 978-0615742113
ISBN-10: 0615742114

Write the author in care of

Catawba River Press
219 WA Harris Road
Morganton, NC 28655-7021

Or email via

www.rlbhartmann.com

Cover photo © by Robert T. Russell
Front Cover design by RLB Hartmann
Back Cover by RLB Hartmann

Prologue

San Francisco, 1917

My locket? Of course you may look at it. Hold out your hand. Pretty, isn't it. I used to wear it, long ago. Ed gave me that little ceramic bowl, and I've kept it in there for fifty years.

I know the picture inside is scratched and faded. Always was. I'm glad, because that makes it easy for me to imagine the face belongs to someone else.

Who? Oh, a young man I once knew....

Chapter One

"This goin' to hurt some, Miss Jessica."

Joshua's fingers knocked against my ear in the darkness, gathering a handful of hair. He gave a sharp tug-tug-tug, and the severed ends brushed my cheek. Another handful gathered up, another painful tug-tug.

Working around my head, he grumbled, "Ol' knife. Never were much account."

It was cold for October in the bayou country. My slippers filled with mud as I crouched beside him in the cane field. On the hill we had just fled down, Federal cavalry streamed into the front yard, yipping like fox hunters, their horses' hooves pounding the earth. The first whiff of acrid smoke filled my nostrils.

"They're burning the house!" I cried, and Joshua's wrinkled old hand caught my chin in gentle warning.

"Be through in a minute, Miss Jessica. A couple more—" He sawed at my thick forelock, the honed blade doing its work. Strands of butchered hair clung about my arms.

"Run get the sheriff! Make them stop!"

"Honey, it too late for that. Now, stay here. Got to go get you some clothes." He hobbled toward the abandoned quarters.

Touching shaky fingers to my shorn head, I tried not to breathe in the drifting smoke. I wanted Mama's reassurance that this nightmare would end. I wanted Papa's firm grasp guiding me by the elbow to safety.

But she had died six years earlier of a fever and lay beside my infant brother in the churchyard, and he had been killed in action, mere weeks ago in the Yankee capture of Baton Rouge.

Until this afternoon, our people—Dora, Sarah, and Mandy as well as Mason and Joshua—had looked after me. But when we had word that soldiers were coming, all ran away except Joshua. With bluecoats in the wide drive, he'd forced me into the darkness, saying, "We can't stay, Miss Jessica. These renegades would harm you."

Now, silhouettes of a dozen riders trampled the lawns, cheering as my home burned. I threw myself prone in the dirt in despair, and felt the thudding hooves beat like devils' hearts in my chest.

Joshua seemed gone a long time before I saw him returning through the neglected cane rows. Sporadic shouts broke through the diminishing roar of flames, and I prayed that none of those men would notice the hunched figure dodging flickering bands of firelight.

He knelt beside me, gasping, "Here's the shirt you got to put on." Disentangling part of a bundle, he didn't wait for my approval but began tearing at stubborn dress hooks, uncovering me to the chill air.

He slid the correct arm into place as if I were an infant. "Step outen them clothes, shimmy an' all. No—don't stand up—"

Pushing at the pale green dress material, then the white linen, I stripped to the skin and shoved first one foot, then the other, into the legs of a slave boy's britches. They were limp with being worn, and though I was small for fifteen, tight through the hips. Joshua set a hat, rank with sweat, on my disgraced head, and I realized he was disguising me as a boy.

"Shoes!" I cried. "What about shoes?" Boys didn't wear slippers, and it was too late in the year to go barefoot.

"I had 'em." He looked about on the ground, found them beneath the folds of my trampled dress. "Here they is."

7

He had socks, too, though the brogans, molded to fit other feet, would give me pain when the wet numbness in my feet was gone. The cloth coat had one button, and sleeves that struck me too short.

I cried afresh for my dresses, cloaks, bonnets, gifts, irreplaceable treasures kept in my bedroom—everything, lost forever.

Bringing out his knife again, Joshua trimmed away the rounded edge of my fingernails. Then he took my wrist and we began running, keeping to the moon-cast shadows of the bayou. Damp earth clung to the shoes, and his grip made bruises.

The dark swamp loomed in front of us like a spirit. All my life I'd thrilled to Papa's stories about ghosts and real creatures that inhabited the low country, and shivered in delight at his warnings never to venture inside. Gazing into its depths, I'd watched a luminous white heron stalk and spear its dinner. I'd listened to the primeval noises and echoes, dreamed of ancient people canoeing its waters.

Now, I thought of snakes and alligators, of slime and things with pinching claws. I could almost feel them clutch at my ankle, twine around my knees. Then we were engulfed in the safety of the cypresses, and Joshua paused so we could catch our breath.

"Don't look back, Miss Jessica."

Like Lot's wife in the Scriptures, I was compelled. And immediately sorry. The two chimneys stood naked, smoke pouring not from them but from fallen, charred roof timbers.

Never again would I skip barefoot along the polished oak hallway, nor eat a savory meal at the damask-draped table in our dining room. No more would I sit on the verandah with a glass of lemonade, nor inhale the perfume from wisteria on a warm evening breeze.

All that filled my nostrils now was the stench of a dying childhood.

He took hold of my wrist again and we set out. Sometimes the path was narrow, sometimes we were soaked to the knees, but he kept me from sinking under the surface or bogging in the treacherous mud underfoot.

"Where are we going?" I asked, for he seemed to know.

"Don' you worry, Joshua takin' you to a safe place."

I couldn't imagine where. I had no relatives closer than an aunt in Indiana, with whom we'd had no contact since the war began three years ago. I might have been accepted into the home of a neighbor, in as great a peril as ourselves, and no better off with crops ravaged; but I no longer had ties to the broad fields and woodlands, and could only follow Joshua. He had been born on our place, so I'd known him all my life. There was no one in the world I trusted more, for Papa had made him our overseer.

We traveled through the night, alternately running, walking, resting. Run. Walk. Rest.

I was near fainting due to unaccustomed effort and no supper, though when we started again I was stronger for an hour or two. Once while we were stopped, I asked, "What time is it?" and he answered, "'Bout midnight." We came across an old corn crib, and I slept inside while Joshua stood guard.

Morning haze still shrouded the elms and poplars when we saw a frame shack at the woods-edge. No orchard or garden offered a meal, but a couple of chickens pecked in the sandy yard. "Do you think we could catch one?"

9

He rebuked me with a look. Numerous times in my life when childish conduct had failed to meet his standards, I'd earned that look. "Miss Jessica, you wasn't brought up to be a thief, and I ain't never stole nothing."

Limping (he because of his rheumatism, I on account of the ill-fitting brogans) we approached the door. He knocked, and we waited, sweating and dirty and weary. How old he looked! Grizzled hair and the stubble of beard, loose skin along the jawline and throat. He'd always been clean-shaven, but the last few days had been chaotic with rumors and then fears and at last the arrival of the enemy troops.

We were about to give up and leave when the door opened a bit and a woman's voice said, "What d'you want?" low, like someone was sleeping inside.

"You need work done? I gladly do it, for one your chickens."

"Got no work. Them's layin hens. You better clear out, fore I set the dog on you."

She started to close the door, but he stuck his hat into the crack. "Ma'am, if you could spare some food, we'd be obliged."

Begging! I knew that hurt him. Not only was the woman of a class below me, she hadn't even Joshua's status. She wiped her bony arm across her mouth like a snuff user. She remained unfriendly, but said, "Awright."

He took away his hat and she shut the door. I didn't believe she would give us anything, and said so, adding, "If she does, it'll be as dirty as she is."

"Have faith, child."

Presently the door opened again, and she shoved a bag into his hands. He said, "Thank you, and God bless you, Ma'am," but mid-way, she shut the door in his face.

The sack was oilcloth turned wrong side out, with a twine drawstring. It contained about a pint of honey with two large soda biscuits crammed on top.

"See, Miss Jessica? The Lord provide. Ain't no call to steal."

Properly shamed, I ducked my head while he said a brief prayer of thanks. Not voicing my fear that a plague was on that household, and that eating food contaminated with it would surely kill us, I reminded myself of the Scripture about the righteous being able to drink poison or suffer snake bite without harm, and sent up a quick silent prayer of my own, asking for forgiveness of my sins, known and unknown. Then I fell to like a hungry puppy. Eating with my hands was messy, but I licked my fingers and waited for him to finish his share.

Two nights passed. We continued traveling west, holing up in deserted sheds during the days, stealing out at dawn and dusk like deer to nibble berries and search for nuts which we cracked between rocks. "Who are you afraid of now?" I asked, as we saw no soldiers, enemy or otherwise.

"The's plenty bad men in this country, Miss Jessica. If anybody stop us, don't tell them a thing. If they ask you your name, you say it Jess. Just Jess, like a boy. You got to be a boy, till we can get where we going."

Late afternoon of the third day, we came to a river and boarded a ferry. "Texas," he explained, digging several coins from his old green coat.

I tried to remember when he might have had opportunity to empty Papa's strongbox. He knew where all Papa's cash and important papers were kept, and had a key. But the last few days and nights were painful to recall, so I sat on a barrel and tried not to succumb to dizziness. The river was neither wide nor swift, but certainly deep, and I had never learned to swim.

The raft, pulled along in jerks by a man working a rope on a pulley, bobbed first to one side then the other, never seeming to advance on the opposite bank despite the brisk hand-over-hand motion, and his tuneless whistle became breathless and finally ceased.

In the silence, the water lapped against the ends of the raft logs. Joshua sat on another barrel and studied the shoreline. We were the only passengers and the ferryman kept giving us curious looks.

At last we reached the landing. "Pleasure," the man said as we climbed the sandy bank. My foot slipped and I stumbled, but I understood why Joshua neglected to help me.

Around a curve in the road, he halted and drew an envelope out of a pocket. "Miss— Jess, you hold on to this here."

"Is there money in it?" There seemed to be several folded sheets of paper sealed inside.

"No, little one, but you ever get in trouble, remember you got it."

The sound of that chilled me. He didn't give me time to question further, but set out as fast as he could walk. I slid the envelope into my coat pocket and practiced swaggering as I'd seen boys do.

The woods thinned and the road widened into a main street, running straight as a plumb line between clapboard buildings, some whitewashed, most not, and I could tell by the rusted tin roofs that the settlement had been here awhile. A few houses, alleys between the stores, a wagon making wheel tracks in the dust.

Destitute people, men and women, loitered on the board walks.

"Are we staying here?" I had never lived in a town, only on our plantation property at the bayou. "Do you have relatives here?"

"No. This be a bad place. We get past, quick as we can. You see a telegraph office, you let me know."

He stumped beside me, bent with rheumatism, worse since our flight through the swamp.

I was looking for a sign marking the telegraph office when I saw the young man on the porch.

It ran the length of a small frame house which someone long ago had started to whitewash. He leaned his chair against the dingy wall, boots propped on the railing, indolently whetting a hunting knife. He appeared to be twenty-five or thirty and healthy, and I wondered why he wasn't in the army.

His battered hat tilted down in front, leaving a lot of brown hair to curl around his ears and straggle about the collar of a faded blue shirt. His brown coat hung open and his beard was not well-trimmed, nor even combed. As we approached, he glanced up.

Chapter Two

His eyes held mine briefly, flicked to Joshua, returned to me. Their touch across the distance (too great to determine color) made me feel as if we had recognized each other, though I could never have seen him before.

There was something exciting about him, hidden like the mysterious depths of the swamp, and I knew instinctively that he lived on the sharp edge of survival. Had I really been a boy, I would have walked up the steps and spoken to him, asking for the tales I was sure he could tell.

His closed lips smiled, faintly, as if he read my thoughts.

Joshua's hand on the nape of my neck reminded me that even without ruffled dimity and ringlets, I was Miss Jessica Linville, of Linville Plantation, Southport, Louisiana. "Don' you be lookin' at no trash like him," he muttered. The urge to turn and smile at the man was strong, but, ashamed to incur further rebuke, I controlled it.

"There's the telegraph," I said. Joshua quickened his limping pace. Going up on the boardwalk behind him, I cast one furtive glance toward the white house, but the chair was empty, a bit askew.

Disappointed, I scarcely listened to Joshua and the telegraph operator exchanging words, until one voice rose harshly. "Get out of here, nigger. I don't send telegrams for the likes of you."

"My money's good." Joshua's words placated, but his manner remained proud. "And it ain't for me. I have to let this boy's uncle know—"

The telegraph operator came around the end of his counter. "Take your money and git. Wasn't for your kind, we wouldn't be in this damn war."

"I got to notify the boy's kin to come for—"

"You're in *my* place! You understand that? Bob, come throw this nigger out. I hear a message coming in."

He went back to his key, and a burly man strode through an inner door.

"I'm goin'— I'm goin'," Joshua said, turning, but Bob didn't stop. He grabbed the green coat near one shoulder and hustled us outside.

Another man passing in the street hollered, "What you caught, Bob?" A third man hurried up, his aspect wild, his accusation loud. "I bet you anything he's the skunk what attacked that white woman in Line Ferry last week. Davy, get a rope and let's make sure he don't see tomorrow."

I grasped at Joshua's other sleeve and threatened hysterically, "I'll get the sheriff!"

The men laughed and one said, "You'll have to go to Cass County to find him."

They pulled us into an alley, their curses and taunts drawing others to the fight. Fists bashed in the old felt hat and knocked it off. I yelled for help—but those who came joined in the attack and blows struck me by mistake. When they forced a noose around his neck, I screeched in earnest. Both of us were trying to loosen the rope when a hand shoved a pistol against his temple.

Joshua threw a shielding arm in front of my face, yet the explosion deafened me and powder smoke blinded me and stung my nostrils, and we fell together. More gunshots sounded fuzzy and far away to my shocked eardrums.

15

The fists disappeared as the craven in the crowd ran off; some stayed to fight each other.

Joshua's weight across me pinned me down, and I knew he must be dead but had no time to realize what that meant, because fingers gripped my arm. A rough boot gave his body a shove, rolling it off me like a meal sack. Hauling me upright, someone jerked me to my feet and flung me onto a tall, speckled horse, then vaulted into the saddle behind me, and I clung to the saddle horn as we galloped like Furies for a woods west of town.

Riding on the saddle forks, my face whipped by the tangled mane, I had no opportunity to glimpse my rescuer. With both of us in the seat, it was a tight fit, his body curving close against mine. I noticed the edges of a faded blue shirt sticking out from the ragged brown sleeves of a coat. The hands on the reins were strong, dirty. And familiar.

It was the man from the porch.

We crashed through underbrush, hit a faint trail, and followed it among a maze of huge trees that grew close and dropped red, gold, and yellow leaves about our heads. Veering, we entered a pine forest, plunged into unexpected little streams without ceremony.

The swift, pounding motion of the horse made my head reel. My riding had been confined to a plush seat in a carriage drawn by a sedate team, so this flight across gullies and dodging marshy places nearly snapped my already raw nerves. Tensed for a spill that would dash my brains out, I clutched the pommel until my knuckles were white.

Eyes closed, I shuddered at the image of that noose around Joshua's neck, his pitifully grizzled hair, heard again the gun blast ending his life, his arm thrust between us in a last act of caring for me.

Tears dripped off my chin and when I wiped them away, my palm bore smears of Joshua's blood. Sobs wrenched upward and found release. I hadn't finished grieving for Papa, and now my friend and buffer against everything unknown lay a corpse in the dust of a town I couldn't name. Nothing I loved existed anymore.

The man behind me said no word of comfort, seeming not to notice my distress. Less and less sun shone through the thatch above us, shut out by great oaks, magnolias, pines, cypresses covered in vines and hanging moss. All manner of lush, exotic flowering plants, just finishing their season, gave the place a rank, wild smell.

At last he drew the horse to a jerky stop.

Dismounting, he reached up for me. When he set me on the ground, my legs buckled and I grabbed the stirrup to keep standing. I was afraid to cry any more, unsure what he might do if he suspected or discovered I wasn't a boy. Everyone in the household had warned me against letting strange men near enough to "take advantage" of me, and now here I was in the middle of a darkening woods, with a man against whom I had no defense whatever.

Though he did not unsaddle the sweating horse, he began rubbing it with handfuls of leaves. As it seemed we were going to stay here awhile, I tried to gather my wits. Nothing was visible in any direction except forest. "Why did you bring me here?"

"You like it better in town?"

His voice was soft, but far from effeminate, with an edge of cynical humor. Our eyes met briefly and I answered honestly. "No."

"That's why."

He cleared a spot of rotting leaves, gathered twigs and laid the kindling, and got a little smokeless blaze

17

going. Then he uncapped a canteen and took a long swallow before offering it to me.

The first gulp burned all the way into my stomach. I held the canteen away, sputtering. "That's vile!"

"It's good whiskey," he pointed out, and took another drink. "Some folks I know would pay a pretty penny for a pint of it."

He rummaged in a knapsack called a war bag, from which came utensils and a couple packages wrapped in butcher's paper. Opening a small sack with his pocket knife, he poured what appeared to be half-cooked beans into a dented pot and added water from another canteen. He started coffee in a second pot. I wanted water badly, but he clearly was saving it, so I decided I'd better keep quiet. He'd rescued me, but his motive for doing so was unclear.

I drew up my knees and linked my arms around them. As the wind freshened, the whisper of leaves sounded like spirits gossiping. I felt awed being exactly where I had wished to be, when I'd imagined myself making friends with a strangely exciting man.

He was slender, muscular, more than a head taller than I, with the easy movements of one accustomed to camp life. The curly hair touching his shoulders had held a chestnut glint in the sun, though everything about him seemed rougher and less civilized away from town. He didn't smile nor exert himself to get acquainted.

"My name's Jess," I told him. "What's yours?"

He bit the inside of his lower lip, and I could see he was making up a lie. "Call me Cully."

My feet were damp, so I removed the brogans and stuck my legs out to the fire. The socks had been rubbed full of holes. I wanted to throw them away, but couldn't keep those clodhoppers on without wadding.

"How'd you come to be with that old man?"

"Joshua? He was one of our people. The only one left. Renegade soldiers burned my home." Fresh grief for all I'd lost choked me, but I blinked back tears. "He was taking me to—my uncle. In Amarillo." The lie came out so easily that I sat pondering what I'd become.

Soon the beans and coffee were sizzling. He gave me the pot lid and a crude spoon twice too big for my mouth. "What's this for?"

"I don't carry any fancy plates," he said shortly. Raking a portion into the lid for me, he added a couple of cold corn dodgers and sat leaning against a nearby trunk to enjoy his meal. The evening had clouded, making the hour seem later than it was. Deep in the thicket, light-footed creatures rustled here and there. The speckled horse stamped a hoof.

I hoped we weren't going to stay here all night.

Cully leaned to push the coffee pot out of the coals with a stick. "He have money?"

My throat ached with bitterness. "If he did, they got it."

"You didn't carry any?"

Thick-lashed eyes, brownish-green in the firelight, met mine as before; only in this setting, fascination gave way to menace. My legs tensed to run, though I knew he'd have no difficulty catching and searching me. "Is that what you're after?"

"Answer me," he commanded, not harshly.

"No. I didn't."

He wrapped the rag around the tin cup and sipped thoughtfully. He left some, and I was glad to get it. "Are you a Yankee?" It was hardly a question, seeing that he wore nothing resembling a uniform.

He gave me a sharp look. "What makes you think that?"

"Only Yankees can afford real coffee."

He laughed, raspy, as if unused to expressing mirth, and began scrubbing the cook pot with sand to clean it. I scraped some into the pot lid and jiggled it around, loathe to put my hand into the mixture. It might be a while before I had opportunity to wash, the way things were going.

He snatched the lid, swiped at it a few times, and threw it into the knapsack. "Put on your shoes."

The half-dry brogans were stiff, so I had to coax my feet into them. Cully went to the horse and loaded his gear. He checked a rifle in the scabbard. Then he came and kicked apart the dying coals with the same thoroughness.

Scratching a few coins out of his pocket, he put them into my hand. Dumfounded, I watched him swing into the saddle. He wheeled the animal, pointing to my right. "It's only half a mile to Linn Flat. They're friendly there."

"You—you're not taking me with you?"

He grinned a little, amusement in his voice. "Now, how would it look, me riding around with a gal on my saddlebags? I got a reputation to think about."

Shock rippled through me. "How did you know?"

"Well, you ain't much to look at yet." He leaned one forearm across the saddle horn and picked at something between his teeth with a thumbnail. "But I knew you was female right off. Any boy your age wouldn't be seen in Dorn's Landing in the company of a nigger."

The word was common enough, but the way he said it made my anger flare. "He was a better man than any of the filthy dogs that killed him!"

Cully's chin went up a notch. "A lot of folks wouldn't see it thataway." Jerking the reins, he kicked the horse and in a leap they were gone, leaving me in a panic.

Exhausted, I wondered whether I could reach Linn Flat before dark.

Cully wasn't out of earshot when he stopped, circled, and came back, towering over me like a prince from a fairy tale. He held down his arm for me to grasp. "Get on," he said gruffly.

Perched on the bedroll, fingers anchored to the cantle because I didn't dare put my arms around him, I got slapped by branches, and pine needles filled my collar.

We picked through thick woods for a good while before we came to a board shack so weathered it blended into the gray-brown forest. Smoke wafted from a pipe sticking out of the shake roof, and lamp light glimmered at one window.

Dusk obscured a couple of small tents pitched nearby. Horses tied to saplings turned their heads toward us, and two men left camp tasks to meet us. Cully stopped in front of the door. "Jump off, boy."

Chapter Three

I pushed my leg over the saddle roll, bounced on the ground, and staggered backwards into the arms of a beefy man with unkempt hair and a beard stained with tobacco juice. He laughed. "What the hell, Cully, you bring your brat with you?"

"He ain't mine!" Cully objected, swinging out of the saddle. "I ain't been tomcattin' around long enough to have a kid that size."

He handed the reins to an old man, and we went into the shack.

The window was covered with tow sacking. A rough table, wobbly on the uneven dirt floor, was across the room from a little cast iron stove. On the table sat a smoky lantern and a bottle of whiskey, and at the table sat two more men, playing cards. The older appeared to be Indian. Neither looked up when we entered.

Cully knew these men well, for he joked and slapped the Indian man on the back and called him Pete. "This is Jess," he said, and then seemed to forget about me. I suspected I was in the company of road agents, and was relieved that Cully went along with my masquerade.

The cabin barely accommodated a bed, a couple of saddles, tow sacks that smelled like potatoes, and two half-grown males warming at the stove. When everyone came inside there were nine of us, unwashed bodies in unwashed clothes.

The combination of sweat, horse, tobacco, and general filth proved nauseating. Needing both warmth and fresh air, I sought a corner near the broken window yet close to the fire. The sandy-haired boy made room for me, asking, "Plan to stay with Cully long?"

"Don't know." I shrugged as if it didn't matter—as if I had a choice.

The other boy was good-looking, ordinarily the sort of person I might notice and be attracted by; but he packed two big pistols in his belt, and his insolent glance made me glad I still wore the ragged coat. For the first time I was aware I'd lost the hat. It was a good thing Joshua had cut my hair.

The drone of men's voices made me long to lie down and stretch out on the bed, dirty counterpane notwithstanding. My eyelids were drooping when Handsome sidled close and remarked, "Young to be a Ranger, ain't you?"

"Texas Ranger?" I knew crossing that river had put me over the border, so it was a logical assumption.

"No, simpleton. Independent Ranger. You ride with us, you better learn who we are. Ever hold one of these?" He drew one of the pistols and twirled it, offering me the handle. "That's a Navy Colt."

I shrank from the weapon, sure it was loaded, fearing it might go off like the one that had killed Joshua. Cully must have been listening. He leaned back in his chair and said, "Leave him alone, Bill."

"I was just showin' him my gun."

"I know what you were doing. I said leave off."

Bill replaced the Colt, and when he was sure Cully was occupied, he squinted his eyes at me in a gesture of contempt. I stuck my tongue out at him, confident that he would have liked to smack me, equally confident that if he did, Cully would give him a thrashing he wouldn't forget.

"Baby," he whispered fiercely. "Piss ant. Go home to your mama." He zigzagged through the crowded room toward the door.

Noticing a water bucket and dipper, I started to it, but Cully's thumb and forefinger hooked my coat. "Where do you think you're going?"

"To get a drink of water," I said. "Where do you think?"

"Hard telling." A little smile touched the corners of his mouth. "Figured you might have a crow to pick with Bill. Wanted to get my bets in, if you was."

"Don't make fun of me."

With as much dignity as I had left, I stepped over men sprawled on the floor in various attitudes of relaxation. The tin dipper was clearly community property, but my thirst was too great not to use it. Cold, sweet spring water revived me for a short while, but as the hours passed, I sat on a bench and leaned against the wall, trying to stay alert.

Next I knew, Cully was waking me, saying, "Come on, Jess. We bunk in with Bill."

I rose from the floor, groggily repelled by its covering of dried tobacco juice and manure-scented foot prints, and followed him into the darkness, tripping on his heels until he ducked into a tent.

A match flared, and Bill held it aloft. "Just checkin' to make sure it's you." He lay on his bedroll, saddle upturned for a pillow. He touched the flame to a stub of candle fixed in the dirt, and asked, "Got any makin's?"

Cully tossed him a tobacco pouch. Hunkering, he arranged his bedding, which was already in the tent. I was preparing to sleep on the bare ground when he peeled off a blanket for me, bumping me with his elbow.

"This tent's made for two," Bill informed me. "Expect to get a few bruises till you learn to duck." He licked a cigarette paper shut and offered it. "Want one?"

"No." I came in a hair of adding 'thank you' out of habit.

"Suit yourself," he said. "Cully, ain't you learned this kid nothing?"

"You could learn to speak properly," I remarked, and Bill's eyebrows went up.

Cully's fingers bit into my shoulder. He shoved me onto the blanket. "Go to bed. I want to talk to Bill."

Wrapping in the scratchy covering, I laid my head on one of Cully's parcels, which apparently contained rocks. Facing the musty canvas wall to avoid the candlelight, I heard Cully say, "How's the cash holding out?" Bill murmured an answer, the rain began, and I fell into oblivion.

Cully woke me before dawn, trying to remove the parcel beneath my head. "What are you doing?" I asked, and he shushed me.

"Don't wake Bill."

I sat up, sensing more than seeing that he was ready to leave. "Where are you going?"

"Never mind. I'll be back sometime today."

"I'm not staying here by myself!" Struggling free of the covering, I clutched it in one hand and his coat sleeve in the other, awkwardly stumbling out of the tent after him.

He shook me off with a curt, "Go back!" but, fearing his friends as much as I'd feared the Yankees, I hurried across the hummocky ground, outstretched fingers in contact with his coat.

The horses were sheltered in a hollow, with the old man to look after them. He stood under a brush arbor, the glow of a partially-hooded lantern revealing his bent figure bundled in a tarpaulin against the damp. He must have known we were coming, as he'd already fed and saddled Cully's horse.

25

"Today?" the old man asked, and Cully replied, "We'll see. I expect so." He stepped into the stirrup but before he could rein away, I threw my blanket across the saddle roll and grabbed the cantle, causing the horse to shy.

"Dammit, Jess, you'll get your head kicked in trying a stunt like that." He got the animal under control and added, "Give him a hand, Preacher, before he makes Apple break a leg."

The old man hobbled forward and grasped the seat of my trousers. That is, he attempted to, but they were too tight, so he laid hold of my thigh and boosted me up. "You need a smaller horse," I gasped, deposited at last on the uncomfortable canvas roll behind the saddle.

"I need less hindrance from you."

He spurred Apple, and we were off into the dim daybreak, breath steaming. Speech came out ragged. "Are we going to Linn Flat?"

"No."

"Where, then?"

"No place you've ever been."

Clinging to the ridge of leather, I let my thoughts range free. I was sure Cully must be taking me to his home. Who would be there? What would it be like? Until I could manage on my own, perhaps it would be my home, too.

My ungloved hands soon became so numb that I had to grab onto his coat. I would have put them into the pockets, but something heavy weighted the one on the right side. Cully said, "Careful. It's got a delicate trigger."

We rode in silence till the sun rose above the horizon. Narrow trails disappeared into the thicket. Crows occasionally called a warning, but we saw no other human beings.

Finally stopping in a tree-sheltered glade, Cully dismounted. Taking a small bundle from the war bag, he unwrapped cold corn bread and several strips of fried fatback. These last months, when any food was hard to come by and Joshua had been forced to trade our silverware for meal and red beans, I'd never sunk to eating fatback.

"I don't like that," I said, accepting the bread with less than delight, pushing aside the meat altogether.

"It's all we got, Miss Priss. Eat it or starve."

His impudent tone reminded me of Bill. "Take me to Linn Flat. People in town must have better fare than this."

He answered through a mouthful of food. "You had a chance to go there last night."

"I want to go now."

"Too far out of the way."

"Where are we?" Our rambles had so disoriented me that I had no idea which direction to turn. Though my heart fluttered just a bit, remembering I was at his mercy, I felt strangely at peace. He might eventually harm me, but he wouldn't let anyone else do so.

"Liberty County," he informed me after a pause.

"What are we doing here?"

"Waiting."

"For what?"

"For mare-lows to catch meddlers. Now hush and let me think."

"What about those men who shot Joshua?"

"What about them?"

"Can't you and your men clean out the lot of them?"

"Not worth the trouble."

"You scared?"

"Of those bastards?" His glance was incredulous. "Cullen Baker's not scared of anybody. You remember that."

I believed him. In the morning sunshine, he stood hands on his hips, coat hanging open, head inclined as if listening. Gaily-colored leaves drifted about us with each breeze, and bird-calls made the scene seem ordinary, but it was far from being that.

Waiting, he'd said.

Tense with not knowing what he meant to do, I was bothered by Joshua's admonition: 'Don't you be lookin' at no trash like 'at.' *White trash* was a term that always made me think of shiftless men and dirty children. Had Cully come from such a home? Joshua had thought so. I didn't dare question him about it, for he might leave me in the first settlement we came to; and I was quite sure that was the last thing I wanted.

Cully stiffened as if he heard something.

"What is it?" I peered through the trees in the direction he was looking. He didn't answer, but there was the distant chuff of a steam engine, accompanied by the dull thrumm of a train passing over rails. "Are we catching a train?"

"I am. You stay here." He snatched Apple's reins from an alder limb and vaulted into the saddle. He was gone before I could draw breath, riding swiftly along the woods-edge toward the sound.

A locomotive came into view at the far end of a field of yellow grass. In a panic at being left, I ran toward it, having some notion of flagging down the engineer.

Eight or ten riders swarmed out of the woods like disturbed yellow-jackets, pistols drawn, and fired a volley into the air. They wore homespun and slouch hats, and neck scarves tied to mask the lower half of their faces. The train slowed, then stopped, and I saw that a boulder had been placed on the track.

There were no passengers, only the engineer and two other men whose hands went up in surrender as several of the robbers dismounted and stepped aboard the open boxcars. They unloaded half a dozen crates, ordered the guards to remove the rock, and the train was released to chug forlornly up the track.

A buckboard drew up from the far side of the meadow, and the bandits loaded their booty.

Cully swung down from his horse, loosened the neckerchief so it hung around his neck, and stood over the strongbox. He drew his gun and put a bullet into the wood adjacent to the metal padlock.

One of his companions knelt, said, "Another," and Cully complied. The kneeling man wrenched off the splintered wood and threw back the lid, revealing stacks of paper money.

Quickly, Cully counted out a share for each man as they gathered round. One by one they caught up grazing mounts and rode away in various directions. Within ten minutes, the deed was done, leaving nothing but the empty strongbox. Kicking it, Cully said, "They'll quit using wood one of these days." Then he laughed and went to get Apple.

Turning, he saw me. "What the hell are you doing here? I told you to stay in the woods."

Chapter Four

I didn't want to admit that for an instant I'd thought he was leaving me again.

"Now that we have money, can we buy food?" A chunk of cornbread and a few swallows of water was not my idea of breakfast, and fright and excitement had left me ravenous.

He lifted me onto the saddle forks, promising, "We'll eat at camp."

The course he set was not toward the shack. "Where are we going? I thought you said—"

"I've got a few stops to make first."

I soon caught on that when he put me in front, he planned to make short trips, dismounting frequently. Coming to the dooryard of a cabin, he left me perched on that tall horse alone. Its head dipped in search of grass, giving me the sensation of wavering on the brink of a bridge, but I clutched tight with legs and hands and managed not to topple off.

The cabin was the same sort which harbored the snuff-dipping woman who gave Joshua and me the sack of honey. I wondered whether she had died of a plague yet. Then a woman of similar age and appearance answered Cully's knock. She brightened at the sight of him, and a smile softened her features when he gave her part of the money.

As he returned, I commented, "I wish she would invite us to table."

"You wouldn't eat what they got on their table," he said mildly.

The next place we stopped was a frame shack that a big wind would blow into Cass County. The rusted tin roof must have leaked considerably, and the cracks where chinking had fallen out were wide enough for a ferret to crawl through.

A dirty-faced boy about ten answered the knock. He looked cold, in a thin shirt, trousers which struck his shins two inches above his ankles, and barefoot. Saving his shoes—if he had shoes—for winter, no doubt. More of the money passed to him. He beamed at Cully and threw a cheerful wave to me. I waved back.

"Consumption," Cully explained, settling himself in the stirrups. "He won't last till Christmas."

I was sorry for the boy, especially because he had to live his short life in such poverty. At least, before the war ruined things, I'd known comfort and plenty and the love of respectable people. "Cully—"

"What?"

"Which do you think is worse—to have nice things and lose them, or never to have them in the first place?"

"You tell me," he said shortly, and then added, "You'd have to do both, to answer, wouldn't you."

"That's impossible."

"Right."

We came to a settlement of three houses together, none looking like it could withstand a hard rain. He parted with more currency at all of them.

When we were on our way again, I couldn't help asking, "What will we do for money?"

"There's ways of getting more."

"Stealing it!"

"How the hell else would I get it? You see anybody around here going to give me a job and pay me a wage?"

"You could join the army."

"And get myself killed?"

"At least it would be honorable."

"Honorable! I ain't fighting for a bunch of rich jackasses over their niggers."

I snapped. "My father wasn't a— what you said. And I want you to quit calling them— what you said. Besides, what you are doing is every bit as dangerous."

"Only if they catch me."

Getting caught seemed to be Cully's only worry. I spent a little time trying to imagine what kind of upbringing he must have had, to produce such a hardened conscience, and wondered how I might go about changing him.

Then we were jumping off Apple in front of our own cabin, which looked more substantial and well-kept than it had last night. Inside, however, the room still stank, dimming my appetite somewhat.

Bill, who had taken part in the robbery, evidently was out enjoying his share of the spoils, as were a couple of the men nameless to me. Preacher came in to help us dispatch Pete's squirrel stew, roasted corn, and hot biscuits. I'd never eaten game other than venison (which I cared little for), and had I not been hollow, might have rejected a rodent—no matter how pretty its frisky tail nor thrifty its winter ways.

After the first bites, savory with flour gravy and herbs, my aversion vanished. The biscuits were heavy, but I managed to put away two of them as well as my share of ear corn. The coffee was good, not thinned with water or other substitute.

When I rose to let one of the others have my place at the table, an involuntary cry escaped me, and Cully stopped cleaning his pistol. "What's the matter?"

I looked at him helplessly. Respectable girls couldn't use the words I needed, to tell him that the skin on my inner thighs was raw from straddling the horse, a fact I'd been too busy to note.

He frowned, leaning toward me, and repeated, "What's the matter?"

"I—I need some—liniment—I think."

A slow grin showed he understood. "Preacher," he called out the open door, "you still got any of that salve the peddler sold you?"

From out near the tents came an indistinct answer, which Cully relayed to me. "On the shelf above the bed."

Kneeling on a shuck-stuffed mattress indented to the shape of its owner, I searched among snuff cans, pocket watches, a straight razor, a few small coins, a pair of brass cuff links. "I can't—oh, here it is."

Taking the little tin to a nearby shed, I soothed my chafed skin, regretting that a bath and clean clothes were a luxury unobtainable here. I hoped we'd move on soon, but we stayed a second night in Bill's tent—roomier without him. Smelled better, too.

For breakfast, Cully warmed up the stew and made coffee. We ate cold cornpone with it. In the afternoon there were showers, and the men came and went, sometimes bringing in an armload of firewood. One of them added a couple of rabbits to the pot; another peeled and sliced potatoes.

Throughout the long hours before suppertime, they played cards, switching partners often. I sat on the low bench and watched, listening to the patter of rain and the masculine laughter. The subjects were unfit for my ears, so it was fortunate that much of their conversation was cryptic.

"Try your luck?" Cully shuffled the cards. He was speaking to me.

Mama had died before I was old enough to receive much instruction concerning men; but she was firm set against gambling. I shook my head.

"Helps pass the time."

"I don't have any money. Remember?"

"Don't need money to play with me."

"The others did. I saw you winning it."

"Well, I'll stake you. How about five dollars?" He laid it on the table.

As playing would give me a chance to study his ways, I accepted the chair opposite. "I never played anything except Authors."

He threw aside the deck in disgust. "Might have known."

"I can learn," I assured him hastily.

"Better make it Black Jack, then." He spent the better part of an hour teaching me how to play. Soon he'd reclaimed his five dollars.

By that time, Bill staggered in, suffering from an excess of strong drink. He was content to snore on a filthy pallet in a corner until the rabbits cooked. I dreaded his waking, for the room was hot and I'd had to take off the coat. However, going hungry these last months had left me thin, and no one noticed me, least of all Bill. He woke surly and stayed that way during supper.

At dusk, Sandy came in and whispered something in Cully's ear that galvanized him into departure. One minute I was spooning in the last of my meat and potatoes, the next I was rushing out of the cabin at Cully's heels.

We'd ridden quite a distance and dark overtook us before he was satisfied to stop. "Well, get off," he said, for he'd put me on the saddle roll when we left.

"We're not going to stay here—?"

"Safer than most places just now."

He started to reach around and take my arm, but I jumped off by myself. "The ground's wet."

"I've got a tarp."

He unpacked the horse and staked it nearby. The night sky was clearing. Clouds scudded northeastward to unveil a waning moon, and we'd be frozen before morning. We wrapped up in a couple of blankets apiece, the tarp keeping us off the damp earth, but wind in the branches showered us with droplets. Shivering already, I wished we were in Bill's tent. Last night, I'd been warm.

"Who are you afraid of?"

"Nobody. I told you before. For certain, not that bunch calling theirselves the Arkansas Volunteers. My men can handle them."

"You ran off and left your men to do the fighting?"

"Didn't run off!"

"What do you call it? You're out where it's safe."

"When the shooting starts, it's easy to hit the wrong people."

He turned on his side, facing away, and I wrapped my blanket tighter around my head and tried to feel sleepy, but my mind churned with confused thoughts. I knew how to prepare teas, do intricate embroidery, select topics for polite parlor talk, paint agreeable landscapes of the bayou.

But I knew neither how to treat a man like Cully, nor how to interpret the things he said, either with his mouth or with those haunting eyes.

Chapter Five

I was in my bedroom at Linville Hall. Mandy was helping me into the peach-colored dress, and Mama's voice came through the closed door, urging me to hurry, as my guest had arrived. I knew Cully was downstairs, ready to drive me to a party in his carriage.

But when I reached the landing, it was Bill who smirked up at me and held out his grimy hand. The other he held behind his back, like he had a present. With a flourish he whipped out a gun and pointed it at me. "Papa!" I screamed. "Papa, save me!"

Then Joshua appeared in the front doorway, saying, "Don't look, Miss Jessica." He tried to shield an open casket being carried into the house by Sandy and Preacher, but they shoved him aside, and I looked over the banister into Papa's dead face upon the satin pillow. Mama was sobbing behind me, and my own sobs sounded loud in my ears—

"Jess, wake up, you're having a bad dream."

Cully shook my shoulder, and I sat up abruptly. "Oh," I gasped, "was I screaming?"

"No, but I couldn't take any chance that you would. Are you all right now?"

"I think so." Wisps of the nightmare faded, leaving me in the deep forest, alone except for Cully.

When he woke in the mist of daybreak, I asked, "Is the law after you for robbing that supply train?"

He gave me a brief, appraising look. "Law around here won't come after me."

"Bill said you were Independent Rangers. Is that like Quantrill?"

"You know about Quantrill?"

"A little." Pushing off my damp blanket, I hoped we would move on. Instead, he went to give Apple a canful of grain. "How long are we going to stay here?"

He must have heard me but chose not to answer. He took a second pistol out of his saddlebag and stuck it under the left side of his belt. The one usually kept in his pocket was already hanging at the right side. He walked out a ways and drew them both, over and over, aiming but not firing. After awhile he finished with that and lay on his rumpled blanket.

Regarding his matted curls and dirty clothing, I imagined him washed and combed, wearing a ruffled shirt and tailored suit and shiny boots. Beneath the trashy exterior there had to be quality in the bloodline.

"Quit looking at me like that," he said then.

"Like what?"

"Like you want something."

Averting my gaze, I said, "I'm hungry."

"Again? Damn—it's a full time job keeping you in grits." After he cleaned his pistols and checked the loads for them, he said, "You stay here." Saddling the horse, he said, "I mean it this time."

"What if a wild animal comes?"

"Get behind a big tree and keep still until it leaves." He added as an afterthought, "Don't run."

He disappeared into the autumn-bright thicket. I hung my blanket on a branch that caught the sun and looked about me. Forest stretched in every direction, full of silence.

Even if I'd been sure of the way, I dared not return to the cabin. The yard might be strewn with dead bodies—Independent Rangers and Arkansas Volunteers alike.

Midmorning warmed up enough that I shed the coat and was lying on it, watching squirrels in the treetops, when Cully rode into the glade, tied the rein to a limb, loosened the cinch, and untied a canvas bag from the saddle horn. He brought it to me, saying, "Here. Didn't think it would take so long."

The bottom of the bag, where the waterproofing had cracked, was sticky. I pulled the drawstring. There was honey in the comb. Unbidden, Joshua appeared in my mind's eye, telling me, *See, Miss Jessica? The Lord provide. Ain't no call to steal.*

My mouth flooded with a bitter taste. "Did you find a bee tree—or rob somebody's hive?"

"What difference does it make? You said you were hungry."

I held out the sack. He took it, uncomprehending at first. Then he dashed it to the ground. "Can't I do anything to suit you?" He strode out of the clearing.

Well, he had left the horse, so he couldn't go far. He might have exciting tales to tell, as I'd imagined when I first saw him, but it was increasingly doubtful he'd ever tell them to me.

I sat on a rock, shamed by my attraction to him, guilty for staying with him when I knew he was an outlaw and scoundrel. Papa and Mama never would have allowed a man like him to speak to me, much less step a foot in the parlor to visit.

Presently I grew so hungry I ate a portion of the honey, which made me thirsty. Approaching the tall horse with misgiving, as I feared being stepped on or bitten, I found both canteens empty.

Sometime in the afternoon a flock of birds made a terrific din landing in the trees nearby. On their way south, they sought a place for night roosting but soon moved on. Apple grew restless. He didn't like being here any more than I did. Papa would have whipped anyone that left a horse standing around in a saddle, so after a bit I got up the courage to finish unfastening the girth, pull off the gear, and drag it aside.

Remembering life before the war hurt too much to dwell on it, though I couldn't help thinking of Papa. He hadn't wanted to go to war. He loved walking the broad fields with me and sitting on the verandah while I painted watercolors. They were never very good, Papa's praise to the contrary. Would I have a home like that again? And time to paint, books to read, someone to walk the fields with at sundown?

Afternoon dragged into evening, and thoughts churned. What if something had happened to Cully? Could I ride the horse out of these woods to civilization? I decided to wait until dark before trying.

Nothing wilder than a jay had disturbed me; yet with nightfall, creatures would begin foraging. Fanged animals like bobcats, panthers, bears. A campfire was supposed to keep them at bay. If it also attracted lawless men, there was no help for that.

A chill settled over the clearing. I turned up the collar of my coat and unbuckled the saddlebag, searching for matches. Amid heaps of soiled clothing, my hand encountered a wad of paper money. Anger flared. He didn't have to steal food. Of course, the money was stolen, too. At every turn, Cully did things I considered wrong.

I set rocks for a firebreak as I'd seen him do, and after using up several matches, got a small blaze going. A wagon length away I spied a big log, which I dragged into the fire, in case I had to stay here all night.

A piercing scream—half screech, half howl, shrill, like a tomcat but a hundred times louder—cut through the gloom. Apple snorted, jerking the rein, but didn't break free. Though I had never fired any kind of weapon, I snatched up the heavy rifle. Trembling head to foot and nearly fainting, I crouched near the fire, trying to point it.

The cry did not come again. I strained my ears for any tread and watched the horse for further signs of alarm. The eyes rolled and the nostrils sniffed the air for some while before Apple calmed.

Gradually, my muscles untensed. The crackling fire shed warmth and confidence. I took my seat on a rock and drew a long sigh, rifle laid across my knees.

A sudden threshing in the nearby underbrush made me spring up again. The barrel wavered toward branches which shook beyond the edge of the firelight. I prayed I'd have the presence of mind to pull the trigger before losing consciousness.

Arms moving like a swimmer's, a man staggered out of the tangle of bushes into the open.

"Cully!"

He stopped, blinked in the relative brightness, and sneered, "Hhmmhh! I'm home." He stumbled toward the campfire and I had a sharp vision of him pitching into it headfirst. But he didn't, and turned to the business of removing his boots.

"You're drunk." Dismayed, I laid aside the rifle and advanced a couple of steps toward him.

"Not drunk enough."

"I was worried about you." Seeing only thorn rips on his hands, I still thought he might be injured and looked for a wound or bruises.

Tugging at the second boot, he began to cry.

My heart twisted in remorse. If I'd accepted the honey without judgment, he wouldn't've needed to drink himself silly. How many times had I heard Papa say, people were never born mean, but turned that way on account of being hurt by someone or facing something they couldn't endure. "Let me help—"

"Get away from me!" He flung the boot into the thicket. Then he lay down with a grunt, legs crooked up, one arm over his face.

He had come to rest so near the blaze that I was fearful he might roll into it while asleep. "Cully, you're too close to the fire." I took him by the arm, intending to drag him to a safer spot. It was like trying to pull up a maple sapling, beyond my strength to accomplish.

Jerking me to my knees beside him, he grabbed my shoulders and gave me such a shaking my head felt like it was attached with string, and when he stopped I swooned against his chest. He grabbed my chin, forcing me to look into his eyes, glittering in the firelight. "Get—away—from—me." He punctuated the order with a shove.

Fortunately, I fell clear of the flames, and sat rubbing my shoulders while he crawled a few feet to settle in a different place. Hurt more in spirit than body, I wrapped myself in my blanket and tried to sleep, rousing from time to time to replenish the fire against intruders.

Daybreak showed me his sorry state in such clarity that I felt bad about leaving him uncovered. His drunken slumber gave way to movement several minutes before his eyes opened and searched until they landed on me. "You still here?"

"You're lucky I didn't take the horse and leave you stranded," I told him, freshly angry at the frights I'd had because of him.

Emptying his pocket of the gun, he shed the dew-sodden coat and laid it before the fire. He ran fingers through his hair to clear it of twigs and leaves. Then he lurched past the edge of the clearing and was gone so long I had thrown aside my blanket to go look for him, when he stumbled into camp and fell prone beside the coals, head cradled in his hands. "Make some coffee, Jess."

I'd never done such a thing, but found the pot and little bag of ground coffee and stood holding them. "What am I supposed to use for water?" During the night I'd suffered recurring thirst.

One arm motioned vaguely. "Creek—"

There was a rivulet about a hundred yards away. Filling the pot, I dumped in a handful of coffee, stirred up the fire and laid on new wood, and fumed in silence. If he'd been gentleman enough to ask for the honey, we could have spent a pleasant afternoon getting further acquainted instead of steeped in simmering anger.

He was set in his ways...but ways could change. Papa had often taken promising men down on their luck, and set them up in the world. A few had disappointed him, but not all. My mind drifted into those increasingly intriguing thoughts of molding Cully into someone I could be proud of.

The coffee turned out weak, but he didn't complain. We finished the honey, neither mentioning the part I'd eaten. When he seemed somewhat recovered, just to hear what he would say, I asked, "What kind of animal screams like a giant tomcat?"

"Painter, most likely."

I'd heard panthers in the forest at home, yet never seen one, knowing only that our people always closed doors and shutters, even on hot nights, until the screams faded into the remoteness of the swamp.

After a pause, he added, "I heard it, too."

"Is that why you came back? You were worried?"

"They like horse meat."

Stung, I made no reply.

With a leer he reached out and chucked me under the chin. "Got your goat, didn't I."

I jerked away, wanting him to touch me, but not like that.

"What's the matter?" His eyes narrowed. "Don't you like riding with Cullen Baker?"

Within the space of an intake of breath, a dozen confidences and declarations rushed through my brain. I wanted to ask for those stories I knew he could tell. Give voice to my dreams of reclaiming my bayou property. Encourage him to seek a new and settled life away from men like those in the camp. Once the war ended, things would stop being so chaotic.

Instead, I snapped, "I don't like being shaken by a drunken thief who cares more for a horse than he does me."

His lips closed in a tight line. When he spoke, his voice held a leashed fury. "Most people know better than to talk to me that way."

"Most people aren't left alone in the woods with wild animals and nothing to drink. You might have mentioned there was a creek, but that never occurred to you, did it." To my embarrassment, I burst into tears.

"Oh, hell, Jess, stop that crying. A boy would—"

"I'm not a boy! Stop treating me like one." Sobs choked whatever else I might have said—and would have regretted saying, later.

"Look," he promised in a softer tone, "we'll find somebody that'll fry up side meat and eggs. How does that sound?"

Getting hold of myself, I nodded, sniffling. "Isn't it dangerous for you, in a town?"

"Not where I'm going."

I didn't ask where that was.

43

Chapter Six

The gray morning became grayer as a fog settled. Leaves overhung the trail, streaking us with moisture. Thick undergrowth indicated woods which must have been cut in the past, and I craned my neck around him for some sight of houses. "How much farther?"

"A few miles."

Though the whiskey on his breath last night had repulsed me, I couldn't help feeling drawn to him. He tried to be kind. He just didn't know how. I realized that having his respect and admiration would bring me satisfaction; and I regretted not being several inches taller, more shapely, and beautiful.

The misting rain gradually turned into a drizzle that penetrated my already damp coat. I heartily missed the hat I'd lost. "It's starting to rain."

"I know that."

He kicked Apple in the flanks and we sped through slapping branches, careening over uneven ground, the thud of hooves on pine needles matching the horse's rhythmical breathing. A stream ran off Cully's hat brim and splashed me. Shortly we came to a parkland of evergreens, and he reined in. "Go ahead. See—there's a cave."

At the edge of the glade was an opening obscured by wild grapevines, no more than two feet high and not much wider. Taking the tarp off his saddle roll, Cully fastened it around the horse and gear. "What're you waiting for?" he yelled above the drumming downpour. "Crawl in!"

"There might be spiders, or worms—"

He strode to me, grabbed my wrist, commanded, "Feet first. No room to turn around."

On my knees, I obeyed, and he slid in beside me, the sides of the cave crowding our shoulders together. He turned to lie on his back, his hat for a pillow, and shut his eyes. After last night, he was probably glad for a chance to nap. The rough wool of my coat sleeve scratched my cheeks, and after a while my ear started to feel numb. I propped my chin in one hand so I could assess him.

This was the closest we'd been, with time to study him without his noticing. His skin looked healthy, if in need of soap. How did one come to such a state? Careless, unfeeling, neglectful. Yet— How much worse he might have treated me! I was merely living the way he lived. He must want a home. I determined to help him change.

Sand clung to our clothing, reminding me of family picnics on the bayou. Where would I be, next summer? My imagination pictured a small town with quiet streets, and a house—a brick house, with a picket fence, and Cully coming in from the fields. Or maybe a ranch, with stock, and I'd be helping out by teaching. I'd always been bright at lessons. If I could determine a proper way to let him know how I felt, building a life together was entirely possible.

Leaning on my elbow caused my neck to hurt. Arm crooked beneath my head, I sought to get more comfortable.

"Stop wiggling."

"I need a pillow. I lost my hat."

"Well, I don't happen to have a pillow."

"Let me rest my head on your shoulder so my hair won't get full of sand."

He opened his eyes, less bloodshot than before. "All right—just keep away from the gun."

"Don't worry," I promised. Without putting my arm across him, it was hard to find a position that would allow me to relax. In trying, I bumped against the enclosure, knocking dirt upon us.

"I told you to stop wiggling."

"I keep falling off."

Suddenly Cully laughed.

"What is so amusing?" I asked, suspicious.

"You're doing it all wrong." Gathering me into his arms, he held me against his chest. His unbuttoned coat flared beside him, and the rise and fall of his breathing beneath my breasts evoked a new but fearful anticipation. Only the thin cloth of our shirts separated skin from skin. I sensed that he was finally aware of me.

What would it be like, to be kissed by this outlaw whose lips were capable of smiling but chose to mock?

I thought of the pale green dress ripped off by Joshua and left in a heap in the cane field with my shorn curls. Smooth and heavy, my hair was my best feature. It would take years to grow such tresses again. How shabby I must look! Uncombed, in a slave boy's clothing, as smeared with swamp mud as Cully.

"How old are you, Jess?"

The quiet question startled me into telling the truth. "Fifteen." I could have kicked myself for not adding a couple of years, though he likely wouldn't've believed me. People always guessed me to be younger than I was. "Why?"

"Just wondered."

His heartbeat under my ear remained steady, but mine skipped alarmingly. I felt lightheaded, as if I'd been swigging at the whisky canteen. Minutes went by. The rain slackened but continued. He was so still and silent, I asked softly, "Are you asleep?"

His fingers on my arm tensed. "Shhh!"

I raised my head. "What—"

He threw me to one side, the gun coming into his hand in the same motion, and scrambled out of the cave in such haste that dirt flew in my face. I heard a wordless shout that sounded like Cully, then a gun blast. Immediately, from farther on, came a muffled cry of someone in agony.

Dazed, I scooted to the mouth of the cave and peered under the dripping grapevine. Through mist and rain and trees, I saw the saddle and pack strewn here and there. Apple was gone, and Cully was catwalking across the glade. He fired a second time before he disappeared beyond the edge of a hollow.

Clambering past the vine on legs that wobbled but kept me upright, I began running after him, dodged as something large crashed through the bushes at me, and heard Cully shout, "Catch that damn horse!"

"No! He'll step on me."

Wild-eyed, Apple veered, trailing the tie rope, but I was afraid to take hold of it and chance being dragged.

Cully rushed up, grabbed a handful of my collar and hair, and cried, "You better start doing what I tell you." He gave me a shake and went to catch the animal.

"What were you shooting at?" I called, my voice weak. His command had held a rage that renewed all my early fears.

"Horse thief," he answered, snaring the rope and tying it to a small pine.

"Oh, Cully, you haven't killed someone!"

Rain streamed between us, plastering our hair to our foreheads. Those sweet moments in the cave were gone, and he was like a different person, yelling, "Don't just stand there, pick up that stuff."

He flung on the wet saddle blanket and saddle, and cinched up the girth.

I carried the saddlebags and knapsack to him. "I didn't see the rifle."

"I'll go get it." He jogged across the clearing and into the hollow. Returning with his rifle, he jammed it into the scabbard and swung me aboard. The contact and warmth of his body made me remember the first time we rode thus, leaving Joshua dead and friendless in a strange town. "Aren't you going to bury him?"

"He might have partners. I ain't waitin' around."

"It's wrong to leave him, like an animal." I'd seen dead people before, but all had been properly laid out in a casket, (Joshua wouldn't let me open Papa's casket when it arrived at the station), given flowers and a Christian service and a headstone with name and dates. I knew that in the war, good men killed each other and nobody called it murder. Knew, too, that horse thieves were usually hanged. But I couldn't escape the image of my Joshua rotting on a village garbage heap, nor the idea of someone at the mercy of the rain and scavengers.

Cully reined in. "If you want to go back there and dig a hole big enough to dump him in, you go right ahead. Only don't expect me to wait for you." He laid hold of my arm as if to force me off.

"Let go." I tried to twist out of his grasp, terrified that he would succeed.

"Then don't be foolish. You can't bury him without a shovel anyway."

We started again at a brisk pace. "Please, let's get a shovel," I said, my teeth chattering from cold and nerves and the jouncing horse. "We can give that poor man a decent—"

"If you don't shut up about him, you won't get that side meat and eggs I promised you."

He sounded firm, but no longer angry. I persisted. "It isn't right to let things chew—"

"Was it right for him to steal my horse? All my stuff?"

"No, but—"

"Besides, I was just shooting to scare him, and the damn fool got in the way."

Relief flooded my tear-tight chest. Of course, it was an accident. Easy to understand how that could happen, with rain and undergrowth blocking his view. "Then you're sorry?"

"Sure."

"Then, show it by doing as I ask."

"I told you, he's likely got friends. They'll take care of him. You want me to get shot?"

"No, but—"

"Then forget it. We ain't going back."

Brooding, I came to see that he had a point. If the dead man's friends caught up to us, we'd be in a fix. After a while, I said, "I'm freezing."

Cully wrapped his coat around me, closing me inside with him. Exhaustion and warmth lulled me, though I was conscious of the gun in his coat pocket.

My head drooped forward, and I caught myself waking up to find the rain stopped, the air colder. As we came out of the forest and loped across a grassy field, overcast sky opened above us.

"What time is it?"

"Suppertime. Does that please you?"

"Yes."

We rode along the outer edge of a three-building settlement, only a wide place in the road but a real place with real people, not a ghost camp filled with outlaws. Spurning Cully's enfolding coat, I tried to look like a boy.

Applications of Preacher's salve had healed my skin, though when Cully helped me off in the livery barn, my legs were feeble as an old woman's. "You're not going to fold up on me now, are you?" he asked.

"Not if I can help it."

He gave Apple into the care of a stable boy, with instructions as to feed, water and bedding. We took the rifle and saddlebags to the nearest clapboard store, which turned out to be a barbershop. Behind the chair was a shelf full of customers' mugs. The barber began stropping his razor, aimed a stream of tobacco juice at the spittoon and nodded, "Afternoon."

"Fellow get a bath here?" Cully asked.

"Right through that door."

He nodded his head toward another room, and I could see into it. Somewhat larger, containing a pot-bellied stove and high-backed copper tubs. A big kettle steamed on the stove, and a nearby table held a stack of towels. A portly man about forty—my idea of a whiskey drummer—pulled suspenders onto his shoulders and bent for his hat.

"Him, too?" the barber asked, and Cully replied, "Yeah, him, too." It was then I noticed he was counting out money, and *him* meant me.

"Cully!" I hissed as the barber rummaged for a mug and brush, "I can't go in there!"

"Sure you can. I won't look."

"What if somebody else comes in?"

"Stop making such a fuss and nobody'll pay any attention. I'm going to have a shave."

Doubtful, I went through, noticing the door had no latch. As I pushed it shut, he added, "Half a kittle, Jess, the rest is for me."

Slipping out of my coat, I picked the tub nearest the wall and turned it so the high end would shield my nakedness. I found a small cake of soap, selected the largest clean towel available, and lifted the kettle with both hands. There were buckets of cold water with which to temper the hot.

I untied the brogans and pulled them off. The grime-stiffened socks followed. Despite the masculine voices beyond the door, I peeled off the rest of my clothes and stepped into the water. A couple of gallons didn't reach above my ankles, but I splashed and soaped with pleasure, managing to wash my hair as well, a feat I'd never done without help. Unwillingly, I recalled lavender scent, thick towels, girlish chatter as Dora or Mandy helped me into my nightgown.

Cully's voice said, in the room. "We got no time for duds to dry."

I peeked around the tub. He looked younger without a beard. I wasn't sure I liked the change.

After the barber left, I said, "I don't want to put on those filthy rags again. Can't we buy new clothes?"

Chapter Seven

At that moment a light knock was followed by another question. "Shine your shoes, Mister?" A boy about ten carried a small wooden box.

Pausing with a boot in one hand, Cully observed, "They need it. How much you charge?"

"Two pairs, two bits. Like a cigar? Only a dime."

"High, ain't it? Here, let me try one." He lit and tested a small brown cigar. Fishing coins from a pocket, he paid, and the boy squatted and opened his shoe box.

"My water is cold," I said. "I want to get out."

"Well, get out. I'm not stopping you." Puffs of smoke billowed about Cully's head, drifting in a pungent cloud to my nose. He began stripping.

Staring at the wall, I decided that I could step out on the far side, wrap myself in the towel, and wait for them to finish. The boy's tuneless whistle reminded me of the ferry man who had brought me to Texas.

"Pour the rest of that water over my head."

The kettle on the floor was cooling. I glanced at the boy, who kept plying his brush.

"You." Cully fixed me with an impatient frown.

Big as it was, the towel wouldn't stay put unless I held it. One-handed, I picked up the kettle and, with my gaze well above the danger level, I did as I was told.

He vigorously rinsed the soap out of his hair, which was still as long as mine after the barber's work. "Now put a new kittle on the stove."

To do that, I had to use both hands. Meaning I must first dress. "Our stuff would've dried in no time, next to the fire."

"Oh, hell, Jess. I thought you wanted supper."

"I do. But these things stink."

Surprising both of us, Cully told us, "Stand up against each other." Seeing I was half a head taller, he went on, "Think you can locate clothes to fit him?"

The boy nodded. Cully said in resignation, "Hand me my pants." He counted out a few coins and the boy hurried off.

"And don't look at me like that."

I had thought of expressing my approval, but his brusque words killed the notion. While we waited for the clothing, he finished the cigar and I sat on the low rim of my tub. It cut into my behind, but the unswept floor was unappealing.

Presently the shine boy brought an armload of folded garments. Not new clothes by any means, but welcome nonetheless. Nice quality—sold to buy food no doubt.

"Here you go, Mister. Hope it all fits. Your shoes are ready, too. Recommend me to your friends." The bootblack gave a salute on the way out.

"I'll be sure to do that."

Cully began toweling his hair. "Now, unless you want a peep, you better mind your business, because I'm getting up."

Sheltered behind my tub, I put on a shirt which was a little too large and pants a bit too tight—like before. I'd been unwashed so long that the clean cotton felt like silk against my clean skin. There were socks as well; but something was lacking. "I need a comb."

"Don't you ever get satisfied?" He searched his discarded clothing and came up with a dirty, broken excuse for one.

I swished it through the soapy water before unsnarling my hair. Even after days of sleeping in the wild, it was an easy task compared to untangling waist-length ringlets.

The boy had brought clothes for Cully, too. No ruffled shirt, just homespun that had faded with much washing. He ran the comb through his curls, ripping out tangles with no regard for pain. Along with the grime and beard, excess hair and tattered clothes, his rough appearance had all but vanished, leaving a nice-looking young man, still possessing an aura of being dangerous, but with a subtle presence of breeding.

"Stop gawking," he reproved. "I don't want to have to tell you again."

"I can't help it. You look decent."

He frowned, unsure whether I'd paid him a compliment.

"Are we ready for supper now?"

"I swear, Jess, I'm going to have to whip you if you don't stop thinking up things for me to do."

Watching him stuff our dirty shirts into his war bag, I commented, "I've never been whipped."

He allowed a smile to touch the corners of his mouth. "You might like it." He stomped into his boots, shrugged into his coat, and picked up his knapsack.

There was no cafe, but a boarding house with a sign which said: *Miss Maudie's Meals. 50 cents.* The plank table was adorned with an oilcloth and the pewter utensils were scrubbed.

The fare wasn't bacon and eggs, but cornbread and chili, with buttermilk to wash it down. The girl who served the dishes was a stringy-haired blonde whose bottom, I felt sure, Cully would have tried to pinch had we not been seated with a couple of men much older and of a refined nature.

She liked his looks, too, I could tell. Turning a silly grin on him every time she passed, she finally said, "What a pretty little boy. Is he your brother?"

In the middle of swallowing a bite, I sputtered, and Cully's hand closed on my arm.

"Is the chile too hot for you?" She leaned near us, full of feigned concern. "I can have Maudie send out some oatmeal."

The fingers tightened, holding me. "No, thank you," was all I could say.

"Well, if you all need anything else, let me know."

"Count on it," Cully told her, and released me.

She was busy with another customer when we left. I was glad to go, though the thought of a feather bed made me entreat, "Can't we get a room at Maudie's?"

"Place is full up. Besides, I want to keep an eye on Apple."

Having grain and fresh water, Apple was doing all right. Someone had curried off the caked mud and woods debris. Cully forked a mound of loose, clean hay into a pile near the barn wall. He snapped my blanket, offering, "Get in, and I'll cover you up."

"Won't hay make me itch?"

"It's not hay. It's straw."

Shedding brogans and coat, I did as he wanted. Though I knew the answer, I wanted to know his response. "What's the difference?"

"You eat hay. You sleep on straw." He blew out the lantern flame. "Now go to sleep."

Blinded in the sudden darkness, I asked, "Are you leaving?"

"For a little while."

Comforted by warmth, cleanliness, and a full belly, I slept at once.

Drifting awake, I thought morning had come, but seeing the glow of lantern light, I believed Cully had returned. I'd opened my mouth to speak when two strange male voices brought me completely alert.

"That's his outfit, no mistake."

"Yeah, well, the money ain't here."

"You think he'd leave it? He's out spendin' it free, like that barber said."

"Said he had a kid with him."

"By God, there he is."

I heard them coming and pretended to be asleep. One of them shook me.

"Hey, boy, wake up. Where's Baker?"

I shrank away from his touch. Trying to seem rough, I growled, "Wha'd'you want with him?"

"He's s'posed to've met us last night. Didn't he tell you he was to meet us in Liberty?"

"No. He didn't."

The other man gave a short laugh. "Bet he's at that bawdy house. Figure we oughta let him know we're here?"

"Shut up. This kid's a tadpole." The first man bored into me with an anxious gaze. "He say when he'd be back?"

I shook my head.

"Didn't leave no—package, for us?"

"No. He never said an— nothing about you, or a package, or where he was going, or how long he'd be gone. Now leave me alone. I'm sleepy."

They glanced at each other, and the foul-mouthed one spat. He wasn't ready to leave, for he stood with his hands in his pockets, but the squatting man slowly straightened and scratched his neck. I hoped he didn't have lice, for his contact might have imparted them to me. One good thing about Cully: he harbored no vermin.

56

"Well, you tell him we was here. And you tell him we'll be at Maudie's place till nine o'clock in the morning."

They went out, leaving the lantern burning.

I was wide awake. Who were they? Why did they expect money from Cully? Where was he? Talk being freer at the slave quarters than in Papa's parlor, I knew—vaguely—that a bawdy house was a place where shameless women lived and entertained men who made jokes about them. Could Cully have gone to such a place? Fury engulfed me. No wonder he wanted to get cleaned up. No wonder he had made sure I was tucked in, like a child.

Jumping up, I paced the length of the barn, striving to bear my humiliation.

Joshua had been right. I had no business looking at trash who would flirt with women like the stringy-haired blonde. Maybe he was with her right now, kissing her and laughing about the "pretty little boy" sound asleep in the barn. How could I have wanted a man like that to care about me? He didn't deserve my notice, let alone my trust and affection. Despite present circumstances, I was still my parents' daughter, and had a good name to uphold. How glad I was that I had not confided my tender feelings and dreams to Cully!

Exhausted from containing anger and worrying over what I should do next, I blew out the light and crawled under my blanket.

I was roused again by someone crawling in beside me. In a panic I cried out.

Chapter Eight

"Didn't mean to wake you," Cully mumbled.

He had thrown his blankets over us, for I could feel the extra heaviness against the night air.

"Two men were here looking for you. And their money."

He burrowed into the straw and didn't reply.

"What will you do about them? They said—"

"In the morning," he pleaded, muffled. He sounded like he did the night he'd gotten drunk.

"Where'd you go? To a bawdy house?"

He jounced up on one elbow and yelled, "Shut up!"

"No! I'm tired of being treated like an unwashed sock, and I hate being left to fend off low-down men like that."

"I'm warning you, Jess." This time he was dead calm.

"What are you going to do—pull out your gun and shoot me? I'm sick of being left alone while you're off with outlaws and painted women. I thought you had a little decency, when you rescued me at the ferry, but I'll bet you were just after my money. You got a surprise, didn't you, when all you got was me."

The rush of speech stopped, and the sound of my angry breathing filled the dark barn.

"Are you finished? Then listen. I'll tell you where I was."

For several heartbeats, I wished he wouldn't. What if he had been with the blonde, after all? But he continued in that calm, flat tone.

"I've been burying your goddam dead man. Now I don't want to hear another word."

A tremor of distaste ran through me at the crude language which fell so easily from his lips; but his change of heart filled me with gratitude. He was good. All he needed was someone to make sure he quit associating with men like the ones who'd come looking for him, and those Rangers at the cabin. He was young enough to change. Already I was having a beneficial influence on him.

He raised himself on his elbow again and fumbled in his shirt pocket. Locating my hand, he curled my fingers around a small metal object still warm from his body.

"I took this off of him. Probably got pictures in it." He settled down once more, adding, "Let me put my feet against you. I damn near froze out there on account of you."

I snuggled against him, and the soles of his feet located my legs.

As Miss Jessica Linville, of Southport, Louisiana, I never would have slept in the same room with a man until my wedding night, much less in the same pile of straw. True, he had held me in his arms, but this was different somehow. The intimacy shocked and excited me. Mama had married at sixteen. I fell asleep dreaming about the small brick house and Cully.

My first thought on waking was that it was light enough to see inside the locket. I pried open the clasp with a thumbnail. One tiny likeness, so worn it wasn't possible to tell if it was a man or woman. "Oh," I murmured, disappointed.

Cully came from watering Apple and hunkered beside me. Taking the locket, he studied the image. "His ma, I reckon."

Something guarded in his manner suggested more knowledge. "What makes you say that?"

59

He picked up a piece of straw and bit the end of it. "Nobody else that ugly."

"You knew him? Knew his family?"

"We wasn't friends, if that's what you mean."

He began currying Apple, and I searched the scattered straw for my shoes.

His callous attitude unnerved me, though I was sure it came through no fault of his own.

Papa, gentle-natured as he was, must have killed men in battles. I'd seen him no more than half a dozen times during the past three years, when he was home on leave, and he wouldn't talk of the war. Although Cully seemed considerably less moved by the events of yesterday than I, maybe he was like Papa, hiding his real feelings. Like me, hiding mine.

Before he had time to object, I crossed the stable and put my arms around him. "I'm glad you went back."

For once, he didn't push me away. "I do the best I can, Jess."

I believed him.

When he failed to return the hug, I released him and groped for a topic of conversation. "You left Apple last night. Did you walk?"

"Don't be silly." He knelt to check his gear.

"You stole a horse?"

"I used it for a little while. Apple'd had enough for one day."

"Did the man who owned it know you were using it?"

"Hand me that sack," he said, and I complied.

"What about those men? Were you supposed to meet them? Do you have a package to give them?"

"Good God! Must you question every move I make?"

"I just need to know what to expect."

He gave me a coin. "Go over to Maudie's and buy yourself some breakfast."

"You come, too. You ought to eat."

"Yeah, well, there's no time for eating. I got things to do."

He was cleaning one of those pistols as he said this, so I started out for Maudie's, but stopped. "They'll be there, and they'll ask me where you are."

"Well, tell them. They don't scare me."

The men were at Maudie's, just as I'd predicted. The minute they saw me enter, both left their coffee without delay. Torn between having a meal while I could, or following them, I paid for a couple of cold biscuits filled with pieces of fried side meat. That was less than a cut above fatback, but I had no leisure to be finicky.

When I reached the stable, the two men were ranting, yet keeping their distance from Cully, who leaned against a stall and answered their accusations as if their bluster didn't bother him. I peeked around the doorpost and none of them noticed me.

"Look, Baker," the foul-mouthed one snapped, "we did our part and we want our share."

The other joined in. "Hand it over and there won't be any trouble."

"You had no part," Cully didn't raise his voice. "and you get no pay. I never invited neither one of you swamp rats in on the deal."

"Word come to us to the contrary."

"That's your story. Take my advice and clear out while you can still breathe."

The older man gestured at his partner, a show of caution, but the foul-mouthed one sneered, "I've heard you think you're the devil hisself in a fight, but I bet we could take your whole damn rig if we wanted to."

"Last man tried that won't try again."

They jumped him so quick I didn't have time to scream. All three were scuffling—they to land a solid blow and he to get to a loaded pistol—when I rushed into the barn and grabbed up the nearest object, an unwieldy hay rake, and raised it high for a good swing.

"Ho, Jess!" Cully shouted, dodging.

His attackers gave startled looks over their shoulders, and the tines of the hay rake struck both of them across the forehead. They fell off to either side, holding their heads and cursing.

Cully would have shot them for sure if I hadn't latched onto his arm, shouting, "Let them go! Let them go!"

He fired anyway, with my fingers grasping the barrel. The men scrambled for the door. Another shot went wild as they gained their feet and freedom. "Damn! Jess, you made me miss!"

"I saved your miserable life!" I cried, holding my shocked hand. "Look what you've done to me!"

Defiance ebbed, leaving his eyes sane, like before. He reached for my hand and examined it. "You're not hurt," he said, but his voice held a note of relief as well as dismissal.

"Not just my hand," I told him.

We stood up and brushed straw and dust off our clothes.

"What do you mean, then?"

Drawing a deep breath, I tried to get things straight in my mind before explaining. He re-loaded both his guns. "Didn't you see the blood on their heads? I've never hurt anybody like that before, and wouldn't've had to now, if you'd given them the money."

"They're trash. I could've done for them if you hadn't got in the way."

62

"Don't worry, I won't do it anymore." I started to leave, still flexing the tingles out of my fingers.

He caught me by the elbow. "Wait."

His hold was light and my sleeve plucked out of his grasp as I kept walking. He followed, taking my wrist. "I said, wait."

We halted in the sunshine of what promised to be a fair, mild day. "No. I'm afraid to stay with you any more. You're too quick to use those pistols."

"It's the only way to deal with varmints."

"Everybody's not a varmint—just the people you know. I'm finished with that."

"What do you plan to do?"

"I'll live here. I can work for my keep." I was talking big, without any confidence whatever in what I said. If there was need for a beginners teacher, or seamstress, or watercolorist in this town, then I was luckier than most. Those were my few talents.

He tightened his grip, keeping me beside him. "You can't stay at Maudie's."

"Why not? Is it one of those bawdy houses?"

"Who put that idea in your head?"

"Is it?"

He released me, struck a stance of exasperation with his head to one side and hands on his hips, and at last said, "You better come with me."

My pulse quickened as it always did when Cully put me on the saddleforks and settled himself behind me.

"You didn't hurt them much," he said. "The barber will pour some whiskey on their wounds and they'll drink the rest, and by noon it'll all be forgotten."

I doubted it would be that easy, and prayed I wouldn't have nightmares; but riding in front gave me a view of the countryside, and memory of the blood on the men's heads faded in the thrill of going somewhere with Cully.

We cantered through old open woods with little undergrowth. In half an hour or so, I spotted a settlement off to our right, though Cully ignored it. Meadows around us were bordered by blackjack oak, pines, sumac, and several species I couldn't recognize. The October day gave me a surge of exhilaration. Woodpeckers, doves, and jays filled the bright air around us with drummings, coos, and raucous calls.

When the sun was high, we shared my biscuits and meat and drank spring water. "Look," he said, pointing to tracks in the moist clay. "Know what made those?"

"Raccoon," I answered.

"Bet you can't tell these." He indicated another set.

"A kind of bird—a hawk."

He searched around to find one I wouldn't know. "How about this?" He held aside a tuft of beargrass and I peered at the impression in the mud.

"Rabbit?" I guessed, for one end was indistinct, with no toes showing.

"Is that your answer?"

I studied the track. He was watching me, and I could feel his boyish triumph. "It must be a rabbit," I decided. Nothing else I knew of was that peculiar oblong shape.

"Naw," he said. "Are you stumped?"

The word was unfamiliar to me, but his meaning was clear. "Yes," I conceded. "What is it?"

"My thumb," he said, and showed me how he'd made the mark.

Laughing with him, I felt we'd come through one phase and entered another. A new and pleasant one.

We rode for another two hours before resting in a glade. The magnolias and ferns, tupelo and moss had long since changed to a drier landscape of pines, maples and dogwoods. Warm autumn smells of dead leaves, cook fires in the distance, and meadow grass curing on the stem to a pale gold, gave me a deep sense of hope.

"Tell me a story," I entreated, as we lay on the ground while Apple grazed.

"Story? What kind of story?"

"Something true. True and exciting. Papa used to tell about treasure, and ghosts, and spells cast by witches."

"You think those things are true?"

Truthfully, I had doubts about some of them, but pretending belief was what made the tales entertaining. "You must have had interesting things happen to you. That's what I really want to hear."

"Interesting," he repeated, thoughtful.

"I know you're not afraid, but didn't anything ever scare you? One time when Papa was young, he said, he was driving his pa's milk cows home from pasture and heard a wagon coming up behind him. He tried to make the cows move to the side of the road, but they wouldn't, and while he was busy hitting them with the stick, the clatter of the wagon wheels overtook him and went right on by—but there wasn't any wagon, just the noise. He said it was like it went through that bunch of cows without even touching them. Because it was a ghost wagon."

"You got to wait for dark for that kind of story." Cully arose and went to catch up the horse.

"I like it better in front," I told him when he started to mount. "I don't get chafed so much." Actually, I preferred having Cully's arms around me to the uneventful view of his coat joggling six inches in front of my face.

It was late afternoon before we stopped. Beyond a fringe of undergrowth lay a field, separating us from a settlement. He stepped down and handed me the reins and a few coins. "Go get us some food. I'll wait here."

Suppressing every objection, I prodded Apple with my heels. I'd never ridden by myself before, and even a walking gait felt out of my control, that if Apple should bolt, I wouldn't be able to stop him. At last we made it to a hitching post in front of the general store, and I glanced toward the line of trees, but of course didn't see Cully.

Alighting onto the plank porch, I tied the rein securely and checked to be sure I still had the money in my trousers pocket.

Inside the store, merchandise was scanty, though late harvest items remained. We couldn't very well bake a pumpkin, or spend time breaking green beans, so I chose four sweet potatoes and asked the clerk to cut slices off a cured ham. As Cully hadn't given me enough to purchase other supplies, I supposed we would return to the cabin soon.

With the two cents change, I said, "A couple of peppermint sticks, please." Those were a luxury I hadn't seen in a long time.

Standing on the sidewalk, I was able to secure the war bag to the saddle. However, the stirrups were adjusted to Cully's legs, and I had to shorten the near one before I could use it to mount. While I was figuring out the leather straps and metal rings, a man came by and said, "Need help, son?"

Chapter Nine

Flushed with annoyance and guilt, I stammered, "N-no, sir. This is my d-daddy's horse and the stirrup don't fit me. I'm fixin' it."

My whole life was based on deceit. That had to change. But how? If we kept living where those Rangers lived, I'd have to go on lying to protect myself from a danger I barely understood.

Cully wasn't where I'd left him.

I didn't see him anywhere in the open stand of pines; but the land was hilly, and a little way into the wood my nostrils caught the faint scent of smoke and I followed it. "Cully," I called softly, "where are you?"

"Here," came the answer from farther on.

He was feeding twigs into wispy flames. I tied Apple and carried the war bag to him. He nodded approval of my choices, then set about preparing the remaining coffee.

After we'd eaten and were resting near the coals in the dusk, I said, "I want to start being myself again. I'm sick of lying to people."

He crunched off a bite of his peppermint stick and acted like he hadn't heard me. After awhile he asked, "How long you been with me, Jess?"

I counted. "Two weeks—I think. Why?"

Again, he didn't respond. It was as if I'd known him all my life, yet I knew nothing about him except what I saw: a harsh, uncultured, magnetic personality dressed in worn-out clothes, living like an outlaw in the swamps and backwoods of Texas. From my first sight of him on the porch until now, his attraction for me had grown into a powerful force.

Scoundrel he might be, but I acknowledged my love for him, and determined to do whatever it took to gain not only his respect but his love.

He stretched out on the blanket, propped on one elbow, shadows flickering across him as one brand flared in the darkness and died again to a red hot coal. "You ready for that story now?"

"Yes." I shivered in anticipation.

"Well, one night, when I was about nine or ten," Cully began in a relaxed fashion, "around this time of the year, I'd been to the neighbors' to take them a sack of walnuts, and was coming home. There was a full moon, so I could see plain as anything, except in one place up ahead, where there was three trees growin' close to the ditch, making a dark place in the road about the size of a wagon bed."

He stopped to fish tobacco and shucks out of a pocket. Then he delayed while he chose a stick with which to transfer fire to the cigarette. When the end caught, he resumed.

"The folks I'd been visiting always told stories about witches and haints and such, and they'd been tellin' them that night, so naturally I was somewhat jumpy, being a kid and alone so late. Well, the closer I got to this dark place in the road, the faster I walked, thinkin' when I reached the edge of it I'd take to running, and get through it in a hurry."

He paused again, and I accepted this strategy as part of the storyteller's art—though I suspected he was making it up as he went along.

"That plan might've worked if somethin' hadn't caught me by the ankle and jerked me flat down in the middle of the road!" He made a sudden jerking motion with one hand, and I jumped in spite of myself.

"So there I was, right where I didn't want to be, with big old trees hanging over me and that ditch so close I just knew something hiding in it had reached out and got me."

"What was it?" I asked, knowing he was waiting for that prompt.

He drew in smoke and exhaled before continuing. "At first I was too scared to look—just laid there like a simpleton with my hands over my eyes, kickin' hard as I could to get free. I could feel the thing like a rope around my leg gettin' tighter and tighter with every kick, so after a while I rolled over to see what had me."

"What? A banshee?" My interest was real, but only to learn what he would say next.

His eyebrows drew together in a quick frown, like I was pulling his leg. "No. I expected at least a devil with horns and claws, or a spook from the Patterson graveyard that was nearby. Wasn't a damn thing but a scuppernong vine."

Laughing, I begged, "Another! Tell another one, Cully."

He blew a final stream of smoke to one side. "That's all I know. It's a bunch of foolishness, anyway."

My scalp prickled, for at that moment, watching the smoke dissipate, I glimpsed a pale shape about three hundred yards distant. "Is it? Then what's that white thing I see, yonder by the edge of the meadow?"

"You can't fool me," he said, starting to arrange his blanket for sleep.

"I'm not fooling. There's something or somebody— over there, watching us."

Taking my arm, he plunged into the tall weeds, dragging me with him, and we lay silent and tense for several minutes, side by side, past the glow of dying coals, listening.

Gradually his hand loosened and he shifted his position to raise himself above the screen of weeds. Fearful of making noise, I remained where I was, half smothered. "I see him," he said in a whisper. Easing one of the pistols out of his pocket, he gave it to me. "If there's more'n a couple, you'll have to do your part."

"I can't shoot anybody, Cully!"

"Hell, not at them—you might hit me. Shoot into the air, so they'll think I got help."

Starting forward on hands and knees, he stopped to call softly, "You have to pull the hammer back."

The weeds closed behind him. Did he mean for me to follow? He hadn't said, and I didn't know. How was I to tell if there was more than a couple?

Straining my ears, I heard only a rustle that might have been made by the wind. The rough square of pale shirt front which I'd seen could belong to anyone—a farmer or traveler, and not an enemy at all.

The woods were silent except for the stream rippling at the foot of the slope behind me. I tried to crawl noiselessly along the trail of flattened grass left by Cully's passage. His pistol weighed at least two pounds, and trying to keep it pointed at the night sky, while making my way toward the edge of the brush, taxed my nerves and strength.

Without the crackle of a footstep to warn me, someone seized the barrel of the gun. At the same time, a hand covered my mouth and a knee landed between my shoulder blades, knocking me to the ground. The gun went off as we fought for possession.

Twisting around, I lashed out with both feet, freeing my mouth enough to scream, but he was astraddle of me, thighs encased in smelly buckskin holding me prisoner, his strong hand bruising mine on the gun.

In the blackness of the moonless night, there was no seeing my attacker. I sensed he was in his prime, virile and muscular, and if I didn't manage to cock that pistol and fire it into him, he would send the barrel crashing into my skull with no more conscience than if I were an unwanted cur.

His grasp enclosed the hammer, and he was near to breaking my wrist when I punched him hard as I could with my other fist. The blow landed well below his belt. He gave a yelp and fell off sideways into the brush.

I heard Cully laugh.

The man lay groaning. Our campfire blazed with new wood, silhouetting Cully as he walked towards us.

"Are you all right, Jess?" He took me by the hand and pulled me to my feet. With his rifle he prodded the intruder. "Well, if it ain't the cap himself," he taunted as the man rolled over and firelight showed who he was.

"I didn't shoot him—did I?" I questioned, confused.

"Might as well have," Cully said, laughing again. "He wishes you had. Don't you, Cap?"

The man cursed, but didn't offer to get up and resume the fight, even when Cully took back his gun. Nor when Cully tied his wrists and ankles with lengths of rawhide.

"Come on," Cully said to me. "We'll go where things are a little quieter." He threw the saddle and gear onto Apple, and me onto the saddle forks, and away we went through the dark forest.

The sun was coming up when we halted.

A homestead which seemed deserted but Cully said wasn't, offered a barn with a loft, so he led Apple into a stall and we climbed the ladder and spread our blankets on loose hay. At last I had to ask, "Was he by himself?"

"No. There was another one."

"What did you do to him?" I hadn't heard any gun, except the wild shot while I was grappling with Cap.

"Not much. Tied him to a tree and carved my name on his chest."

A dart of fear gave way to the suspicion that he was joking. Still, I knew he carried a sheathed hunting knife, so dropped the subject before he told me more than I wanted to hear.

"Jess," he said, lying relaxed on his back an arm's length away, "don't ever hit a man where you hit Cap unless you plan to do some damage."

"Why not? It was effective." I could've added that Cap certainly planned to do me some damage.

"Because it hurts like hell, that's why not," he said.

I wondered who had hit him like that, but said only, "Are they friends of yours? If they are, I'd hate to meet your enemies."

"Friends! They're bounty hunters. If you hadn't been—"

In the silence, I gathered that my presence had saved the lives of those men last night. Maybe Cully included. Having been praised and cherished all my life, I badly needed approval and nurturing from him, even if I had to ask for it outright. "I helped you out, didn't I?"

"Well, they won't forget it."

When we'd finished our sleep, he went to the farmhouse and brought back soda biscuits, chunks of stew beef still steaming and moist with broth, and a bag of pears. Picnicking in the loft with Cully was more enjoyable than fishing for catfish in the channel with Joshua.

"You called him Cap like you know him."

"I know him. He's one of them Volunteers I told you about."

"You've fought with them before?"

"They've tried to hang me."

"Is there a reward out for you?"

"Not yet, but I reckon there will be, one day. No, it's more like a feud. Something starts it, and next thing you know it's all built up till somebody gets killed. We're way past that point now, so it's just a matter of time."

I grasped the wedge I'd been needing. "Why don't you leave this country, and go somewhere new?"

"I got obligations here. Besides, I told you, I'm not afraid of those bushwhackers."

"I am." I shuddered, recalling the smell and feel of the man in buckskin.

We spent the rest of that day in the loft, matching pennies and finishing the beef. I told him what I could remember about Mama and how close Papa and I had been and what good times I'd had with Joshua and Mandy, Dora and Jason, and the others—before the war started, and everything changed. "Why do people have to fight!" I cried; but he didn't answer.

By now I loved him so much I thought it must show. I yearned to sleep close and secure in his embrace, yet reluctantly decided that such intimacy would have to wait for the minister and a certificate of marriage.

Waking, I heard Cully moving about below, the clink of a tin pail as he watered the horse. I rolled my blanket inside Cully's—he'd left it in disarray—and tied them with a strip of rawhide.

Peering over the loft edge, I watched him check Apple's shoes, pat the speckled neck, and measure out grain. "Good morning," I called, and he glanced up.

"Mornin." Sounding serious, he added, "I want to talk to you."

In a moment I was beside him, the bedroll under my arm, noting how he wouldn't meet my gaze. "Talk away," I encouraged, inwardly nervous.

73

He leaned his forearms across the top board of Apple's stall, so all I saw was his profile and not the truth in his eyes. "You came close to getting killed the other night."

Any regret I might have had at causing injury to my attacker left me. "You didn't show much concern then."

"I've had time to think about it."

There was a long interval while he seemed to discard part of what he had meant to say. "You were right about me being after your money, but it wasn't the only reason I got you away from that crowd at the landing. I didn't want to see you get hurt—and I still don't."

The sound of a distant door closing reminded me there were people living near. Events of the previous nights were no more than dream fabric now. "Nothing can hurt me as long as I'm with you, Cully."

"There's where you're wrong." He swung around and something like anger shone in his eyes. "I've seen game females before, but you're too bold for your own good."

Not sure how to react, I said, "Well, I guess if I wasn't, that bounty hunter would've bashed my head in."

We glared at each other for several heartbeats. "What are you getting at?" I demanded.

He threw up his hands, then commenced readying Apple for a ride.

"Where are we going now?"

"A friend's house. Widow, name of Loring."

Thank God, I thought fervently. *A house, with a woman in it.* I figured my time of the month wasn't far away, and providing for that event was lately a recurring worry. Too, I was curious to see her, having once heard a bunch of drunken soldiers at the depot sing a dirty song about a Mrs. Loring, though I didn't suppose she would be the same one.

About mid-morning we came to a tidy settlement, colorful with big trees in autumn foliage. The road ran straight through town, with perhaps twenty homes and as many stores. Yards were shaded and fenced. I noticed there weren't many people on the streets, but things looked pleasant.

We turned in to the last house, where a black boy about eight or nine was skipping around the trunk of a big willow. When he saw us at the gate, his face blossomed with gladness. "Mist' Cully!"

"Mack, go fetch Mrs. Loring."

The child raced into the house, letting the door slam. Dismounting, Cully said, "Get off by yourself. Don't let her suspect you're not a boy."

By that time, the widow stood on her porch, hands propped on corseted hips. Tall and big-bosomed, she had salt-and-pepper hair braided across her head. Her dark blue crepe dress was too tight, as if she'd put on weight and lacked money for a new one. Her expression was impassive. "I see the Yanks haven't captured you yet."

We went through the gate. "Rebs, neither. This is Jess. Can you feed us?"

"Ever know when I couldn't?"

Chapter Ten

She showed us into the front room, small and dark, with respectable furnishings. I surmised that she and Cully were friendly, but she never smiled as if happy to see us. Mack, on the other hand, dashed down the hall to the kitchen, where he began pulling out baskets of potatoes and turnips, and a ham wrapped in sacking.

Cully sat at the table and took off his hat. He looked lean and tired, and no wonder.

The widow directed the little black boy to put away his misguided offerings, then she set out mugs and cider, and stirred a pot of something on a stove that was humming, all the while spouting gossip and politics about which I knew and cared nothing. I hung the ragged coat over the other chair and went to the washstand.

"The boy has better manners than you, Cully. At least he knows enough to wash."

Accepting a mug, he moved to rest one ankle across the opposite knee. Money for the shoeshine had been wasted.

Mrs. Loring continued to lambaste the Federal Army as she sent a small boy's shirt on vigorous trips up and down a washboard. Her tirade and splashings concluded simultaneously. Giving the garment a final squeeze, she slapped it onto a pile of rinsed laundry, said, "There!" and handed the basket to Mack. "Now you hang them right this time," she admonished as he staggered out the door.

She sat with us, complaining, "Last washday I had to do them twice. He didn't use enough pins and the wind scattered things all over the yard." Her hand wiped ineffectually at a strand of hair. "Soup'll be ready soon."

"You could use more help around here," Cully remarked.

"Lord knows, that's the truth. It's hard, trying to keep body and soul together with pickings off that wore-out vegetable patch. And keeping wood on the place and split. He's too little to handle a axe."

She stood with a quick movement, halting with a cry and grabbing her shoulder. "Rheumatize is worse. All that rain we had."

That explained why she preferred working indoors and roasting to doing her wash in the yard on a pretty day. I mopped beads of sweat off my forehead and sat hunched, hoping she wouldn't question me.

She dished up heaping bowls of soup and gave us each a big wedge of cornbread. "Coffee, Cully? It's real."

"Won't pass that up."

"Don't I get any?" I asked, needing it in spite of the heat.

"Coffee sallows the skin," the widow commented, but filled my empty cider mug with the observation, "Guess boys don't worry much about such like."

Cutting my eyes toward Cully, I wanted to convey glee at fooling a shrewd old lady like Mrs. Loring, but he concentrated on his bowl and I commenced eating with good appetite.

Their talk of people they knew, recent happenings, and the state of the economy, interested me less than the idea that we would stay here and provide her with the help she needed. Cheered by the prospect of sleeping in a bed again, having regular meals, walking streets which would become familiar, and making friends, I wasn't prepared for what followed.

Cully pushed aside his dishes and reached for cigarette makings. "Mrs. Loring, I would like to leave Jess with you."

My heart lurched.

"Well, he's kind of puny," she answered slowly. "If you could pay me a little something, I'll look after him for you, and won't work him too hard."

That sent my hair crawling up the back of my head. Work me, indeed! Like that poor little field hand, loaded down with wet laundry, stretching to reach a line high enough to hang her dresses. I recovered enough to tell them, "I'm not staying."

Cully's jaw tensed, and I knew immediately that blunt rebellion was not the way to handle him. Ignoring me, he said, "No need to work him at all. I got money." He drew several folded bills out of a pocket and handed them to her.

She fingered the paper. "That the best you can do?"

Grudgingly he gave her a gold coin that looked like a double eagle. So much money would pay for months—years! What was he doing to me?

Accepting the coin, Mrs. Loring left the room, no doubt going to place it in a secure spot.

"Cully! Don't leave me here! What if she finds out I'm a girl?"

He fixed me with an intense look and warned, "You better not let her."

He said it like a threat, making me think there was more to consider than how irate she might be if she learned we'd tricked her. I leaned across the table and grabbed his hand. "You will come back for me, won't you? I want to be with you."

"Well, you can't."

"Why not? I'm not afraid."

"You should be." He shook me off as we heard the widow's steps in the hall.

"I'll need supplies and ammunition," he told her.

"I don't know what's left down there. You can look if you've a mind to."

The boy had finished at the clothesline. Cully gave him the last draw from the cigarette and said, "Come hold the light, Mack."

I jumped out of the chair and would have gone after them, had not Mrs. Loring stood in the way. "Where'd he find you?" she asked, curious but not unkind.

Snatching the name out of thin air, I blurted, "Liberty."

"That's a ways from here. Been with him long?"

"No, Ma'am. A few days."

"How'd you meet him?"

I remained standing, intending to rush out the front door as soon as I saw Cully pass the window. I'd make such a scene he'd have to take me with him, or draw the neighbors' attention—and I was positive that was the last thing either of them wanted.

"Um. There was a—brawl, and my—uncle was—killed. Cully let me—ride with him."

"He's like that. Good hearted." Her eyebrows frowned as she massaged her shoulder. "Howsomever, that's no life for a boy your age. Trouble follows him like a shadow. He's showing good sense, bringing you here. I don't have much, but I don't mind sharing. Mister Loring, God rest his soul, always wanted a son, but we never—"

Mack came in, carrying a tow sack. "He gone."

I tore through the hall, nearly knocked over a lamp in the front room, threw open the door so hard it banged against the wall—but I was too late.

79

Deep hoofmarks marked the sandy road, so he'd left in haste. I followed the trail past several homes, until it veered into the forest. I stood gazing at the brushy undergrowth, figuring out that he'd slipped around the other side of the house. How crafty he was, to have understood me so well, and elude me so easily.

Fighting despair, I told myself I must not cry. I must stay at Mrs. Loring's house, and wait for Cully.

The widow acted as if nothing had happened. She set about peeling Winesaps. "Cully ride all night?"

"Most of it," I mumbled, longing to rest somewhere by myself. Would I have to sleep with the little black boy? Or would my bedfellow be the formidable widow herself? How long could I keep up the deception which seemed so vital to Cully?

"Then you should nap till dinnertime."

She steered me down the gloomy hallway and up the creaking staircase. At the landing, doors opened right and left. She put me in the front bedroom, wherein were a narrow iron bedstead covered with a fat mattress, a maple washstand, and a walnut dresser. She crossed the floor to shut chintz curtains, making the cold room dark except for the faint glow around the top of the window.

"Get between that quilt and the coverlid," she instructed. "I don't want you on the sheets till you've had a bath."

"Yes, Ma'am." With a pang I realized that living here was going to present one danger after another to my masquerade.

'Dinnertime,' was the noon meal, though it was closer to two when a presence in the room brought my eyes open. Mack stood just inside the door, holding a bundle. Seeing that I was awake, he held it out. "Miz Lorin' say come eat."

The garments were still warm from a hasty drying in the kitchen. My slave clothes, freshly laundered, the shirt patched where I'd ripped it while Joshua and I were yet unpracticed in crossing under nailed plank fences.

Regretting that the coat was too bulky to be washed, I laid the things on the bed and went downstairs.

The fare was soup again. My hunger had vanished, but I ate a small piece of the pie she gave me.

"Waterbucket's empty," she told Mack.

"I'll go," I offered, needing to escape the furnace-like kitchen and the reminder of Cully's empty chair. It was a bit askew, just like he'd left the one on that porch.

Mrs. Loring said, "You don't need to. Remember, Cully gave me enough for your keep."

Paid to be rid of me, I thought uncharitably; but at once assured myself that he thought my being with him was dangerous. He'd taken supplies and ammunition. Evidently planning a new escapade. Soon as it was done, he'd come for me.

"I want to."

The back yard was flat and sandy, edged in scant grass and a tangle of established honeysuckle, oaks with leaves that clung when cheerful old maples cast theirs off with every breeze. Beyond was a sloping, weedgrown field and woods beyond that.

The windlass sat on a hump of bare ground at a moderate distance from the house. Letting down the bucket, I could see the road where Cully and I had ridden up and dismounted. Obscured by oaks, hedges, and fences, were small whitewashed houses. They didn't look so friendly now.

When I went in, sniffling, Mrs. Loring noticed but all she said was, "I told Mister Loring when he built this house, he should put it nearer the well, but he wouldn't. He liked to sit on the porch and watch goings-on in the street. Don't you have a handkerchief, child? Here." She gave me a clean one from her dress pocket.

"It's not safe to sit on the porch nowadays, what with the Yankees riding into town whenever they feel like it. You'd think that bunch of Rebs up at Marshall would come clean them out, but they never do. I think they're afraid they'll stir up more trouble than they can handle."

Mrs. Loring's shoulder got to bothering her so much, she had to go lie down. Mack was put to shelling a bushel of dried peas; so clearing the table and washing the dishes became my job. The activity helped ease the turmoil in my mind, though I speculated on where Cully had gone. Who was he with? What was he doing? Was he thinking of me? Missing me?

Tonight, when he ate a lonely supper with no Jess to smile at him over the campfire, he would miss me.

Comforting, too, to know that he and the widow were friends. He must stop by sometimes. Now that I was here, he'd want to be sure I was treated well, that his money was receiving full value.

Putting away the dishes, I asked, "Want help with those peas?" and Mack flashed me a shy grin. I contrived to start him talking. "You like Cully, don't you?"

"Suah do. He give me dis." He extracted a buckeye from his trousers pocket and handed it to me.

I nodded and smiled, pretending to admire the present. "Does he come here a lot?"

Mack shook his head. "He always down inda swamp. Too many sojers aroun' here."

Disappointed, I fell silent, shelling and dreaming.

By evening, my back hurt and I wanted to walk up the street to see what the town was like, but Mrs. Loring sent me out to play ball with Mack. It was better than nothing, so I amused myself with that awhile, and then helped him carry in stove wood. If the widow herself had chopped all this, no wonder her shoulders ached.

My bath in the kitchen was unattended—thank God—and clean clothes made me feel better, though I was reminded of the cozy warmth and banter in the barbershop with Cully, and a few tears fell.

Supper was pork chops, gravy, and biscuits, with green beans and potatoes cooked together. After Mack and I tidied the kitchen, we joined Mrs. Loring in the front room and she got out her knitting.

"I'm working on a shawl." She smoothed the rumpled end to show me the colors and design. "I been at it about four months, expect to finish around Christmas."

I wondered if I would be here at Christmas.

Chapter Eleven

Mack brought a board and a box and begged me to play with him. "Checkers," he said, laying out the pieces of a game I knew as Draughts.

He wasn't a very good player, becoming upset when I won. Mrs. Loring sent him for a glass of water, and told me, "He's a bit simple, Jess. You be a good boy, and treat him nice."

The word *boy* struck me like a slap, but if she noticed my flinching, she thought it was because I had to let Mack win. He was so pleased at taking my 'kings' that he kept me playing till bed time.

"Will I sleep in that same room?" I asked, putting away the game.

"Yes. When Mister Loring was alive that was our bedroom, but after he passed on I just couldn't rest in there anymore."

"Is Mack across the hall?"

"No, he has a cot in the storeroom off the kitchen. That reminds me—" She turned to the child and fired a question at him. "Rats getting into the boxes yet?"

"No'm."

"Can't let them get started. Our winter stores keep us going, when Cully—. I used to keep a lodger in that back room upstairs, and if I still had the furniture, might do it again, but you can't trust folks these days. No telling who you would get, or whether you'd be paid or killed in your bed."

Next morning, she said abruptly, "I can't abide looking at your shabby feet. We'll chance a trip to the mercantile. Cully paid enough, I think I can get you a pair of boots."

"New boots?" Footwear cost plenty, as did real coffee, flour, dress goods, and other articles I'd learned to do without. "Is the war different here, then?"

She gave a mirthless laugh. "I expect it's the same everywhere. You just have to know the right people."

"Oh. Is the owner a friend of yours?"

"No. Cully is."

That was all she meant to say, for she hustled us up the street and into the store. The boots were a bit too large, but Mrs. Loring said, "I can knit him a pair of socks that'll fix that."

I wanted to throw the brogans away, having had my fill of them. "Mack'll grow into these." She handed him the shoes. "We don't waste anything."

We came out onto the board walk. Wagon tracks in the street showed evidence of life, but little was happening to prove it. I craved diversion. "May we look in a few more stores?"

"Not much to look at. But we'll go. Satisfy your curiosity, and we won't have to bother again."

Before the war, trips to Mobile and Shreveport, Natchez and Vicksburg had always been excursions of adventure and excitement. So many new things to see, to buy.

Here, morose shopkeepers leaned in their doorways or perched on stools behind meagerly-laden counters. Shipments were erratic or nonexistent, goods no longer being produced, or destroyed or confiscated en route by both armies.

When necessities were bought up by people who could still afford inflated prices, shelves remained bare. Luxury items waited for customers who never came. I walked among the aisles, peering into half-empty kegs of nails languishing for a builder. I read labels of patent medicines.

Fingering dusty lengths of satin hair ribbon, I sighed for my waist-length tresses, trodden into the bayou mud. Homesickness eddied through me.

Outside, the air rang with the strikes of the blacksmith's hammer, but the cafe at the stage stop was boarded up.

"Sad, isn't it," I commented, unthinking.

"Where are you from, Jess?" the old lady inquired with avidity. "You don't talk like a common child. Your folks must have been well-to-do."

I muttered, "They were," and crossed the street. She and Mack followed. We looked into the windows of shops all the way to the end of the block, then re-crossed the street and were back at Mrs. Loring's gate.

"What happened to them?"

"All killed."

"I'm sorry," she said.

Her pity would make me hurt more than I already did, so I shrugged it off and ran into the house.

She sent us back outside and put us to work washing the downstairs window panes. "You might fall if you try to clean the upstairs," she said, so they remained filmed with years of dust. It was mindless work, giving me time to think. To feel. I longed for the war to end, so I could go into a store and buy a new dress, slippers and hat, all at once.

My first day without Cully stretched endlessly from dawn to dark, and I was glad when bedtime came and I could retreat once more, provided with one of Mr. Loring's nightshirts, to the room which had become my temporary home.

One day we went into the woods and picked wild grapes. I laughed, remembering Cully's tale about the scuppernong vine. "What's humorous?" The widow asked.

"Just a story Cully told me."

"I'm surprised he knows a story that would make a body laugh."

Mack and I squeezed juice from large, slippery bags of fruit until nothing was left inside but dry seeds, hulls, and a bit of pulp. A teetotaler, Mrs. Loring cooked down the liquid and made pretty little jars of jelly. She never mentioned where she got the sugar for it, but I suspected Cully's influence.

We sealed the jars with wax and stacked them on pantry shelves, beside containers of preserved meat, honey, and dried plums. On warm dry days we went nutting and filled sacks with walnuts and hickory nuts. "Lord, look at all the acorns!" she lamented once. "I wish I had a hog."

"Maybe Cully will buy one for you," I said, hoping to open that line of conversation. We hadn't talked of him since the boot incident.

"He would," she assented, "if I asked him."

"Do you think he'll come back soon?"

"No telling. He comes when he feels like it, and leaves the same way. A body never can tell when he's likely to show up."

"Have you known him a long time?"

"A few years. He's not easy to know."

On Sundays, she took Mack and me to church services, where the congregation consisted mainly of women, with a few children younger than myself and three or four old men who were past soldiering.

I lived in constant dread that someone would prove more astute than the widow, particularly since an abundance of good food was causing me to fill out; and when neighbors dropped by with news of the war, or children came to play with Mack, I made myself scarce. She would hardly appreciate being made a fool of—introducing me to friends as 'a poor, unfortunate boy' left in her care—and I'd be thrown into the street without ceremony.

At least one of my problems was solved at the end of the first week.

Mrs. Brittain, also a widow approximately the age of Mrs. Loring, came calling with another lady I'd never seen.

"It's terrible," she said as they seated themselves and accepted glasses of spearmint tea. "There's been real bad fighting someplace to the north, and we need bandages right away."

"Lord, I don't have any sheets left," Mrs. Loring told them. "But if you can find any, the younguns and I will be glad to help."

For three days we cut and rolled bandages for the wounded soldiers. The pads I took were not missed, and came to my hand just in time to prevent an accident common to females, that I wouldn't've been able to lie out of. I thanked Providence for supplying my need, and my faith was strong. Cully would show up any day.

Each night, we relaxed in the front room, she with her knitting or mending, Mack and I with the game board. Her topics ranged from sewing tricks to the trickery going on in both governments, monologues requiring simply an 'mmmMMM' or a shake of the head, or a glance, to indicate understanding and sympathy. Mack did his share. Both of us must have looked comical, sprawled on the floor with our game, agreeing sagely with whatever pronouncement she made.

She talked a great deal, and I stopped listening. I imagined Cully's return, needing more and more to see him, hear his voice, have him touch me—even roughly. I wouldn't mind living the life of a pioneer, if there was a homestead with Cully's name and mine on the deed.

Invariably, before retiring, the widow read aloud a passage of Scripture, never suspecting that my thoughts were less than pure. Last, she checked to make sure the outside doors were bolted.

In the fourth week, her chatter got my attention. "I declare, Cully's little wife puts up with a lot. If my man had been the kind to run the swamps, I'd've up and left him."

The words hit me with the impact of banging into a door frame in the dark. "What?"

"I said, if Mister Loring, God rest his soul, had went off for weeks at a time, like Cully does, I'd've left him. My nerves wouldn't stand for it. But she don't seem to mind."

My arms weak, I dropped a checker which rolled across the carpet and bounced against Mrs. Loring's shoe. Mack scooted to retrieve it, and I heard her going on about Mr. Loring-God-rest-his-soul, but my chest and throat ached and my voice sounded thin when I managed to ask, "Cully is married?"

"Well, yes, though you'd never know it, the way he treats her."

This can't be happening, I thought. *I'm asleep and dreaming.* "What does—she look like?"

"Never seen her. She lives somewhere east of here, place called Line Ferry, I believe. Let's see... I'll think of her name in a minute—" The knitting needles clacked three or four times in the silence.

I was afraid my supper would come churning up in a dark flood of bile and bitterness. All I wanted to do was creep upstairs into that cold, dark room.

"Martha!" she exclaimed, pleased. "That's it. She was a Foster. I'm kin to some Fosters on my mother's side, but that's a different branch. I keep telling—"

Unsteady, I stood, ignoring Mack's puzzled look as we were in the middle of a game.

"Going to the outhouse? Better take your coat. It's nippy out there."

"No, Ma'am—I'm—tired. Think I'll turn in now."

"Never get too tired to hear the word of the Lord," she said firmly, reaching for her Bible.

The moment the final sentence released me, I lit a candle and stumbled along the hall and up the chill-swept stairs with the creaky movements of a ninety-year-old woman.

Closing myself in, I shivered out of my clothes and into the icy folds of the night shirt. I drew a breath deep enough to blow out the flame, but my gasp turned into a stifled sob.

All my dreams had disintegrated with that one hated word. *Wife.* He belonged to someone else. Any hope of winning his love was lost, any declaration of my love was forbidden.

I crawled between the fresh sheets and lay curled up, waiting for warmth that didn't come. It was as if he had died and the feelings I had for him would remain forever inside me, denied release. Not only could I never share them with him, neither could I ever admit to anyone what a fool I'd been.

Then hope surged. It was a tale Cully had told for an obscure reason of his own, like making believe I was a boy. Mrs. Loring hadn't met her, hadn't seen her. Because she didn't exist!

He'd told me himself that he had no home. Not once had he said, 'Martha said this,' or 'My wife thinks that,' or even, 'Women are all alike,' showing he had knowledge of the gender. Surely a married man would

90

give an indication of the fact, however slight, however unintentional.

I clasped that hope as a drowning man clings to a willow branch.

Chapter Twelve

Despite efforts to comfort myself, I spent a bad night, tormented by dreams of trying to find Cully in the swamp. I knew he was just ahead, but was unable to catch any sight of him through the tangle of vines and palmettos, hawthorn and sassafras. Once, I thought I heard a gun blast and strove to run forward, but icy mud encumbered my brogan-clad feet, while alder limbs snagged my long and tangled hair.

Waking exhausted, I yearned to stay in bed, but if the old lady suspected an illness she would dose me with bitters. I dragged myself from under the covers, put on my clothes, and went to breakfast.

She glanced at me. "You look peaked. Didn't you sleep well?"

"I dreamed a lot." Served with scalded milk and sweetened with sorghum, the mush seemed to clog my throat. Forcing speech past it, I had to know: "Is Martha pretty? Did anybody ever see her?"

Chewing, Mrs. Loring pondered. "Why, I don't recall anybody ever saying, exactly. Cully's only mentioned her once or twice."

That refreshed my confidence. If no one had seen her, it was because she lived only in Cully's imagination. To reinforce my theory, the next time Mrs. Courtney came to call, I waited till Mrs. Loring was out of the room, and asked, "Does Cully ever visit you when he comes to town?"

Mrs. Courtney's eyes widened in positive alarm. "Adelaide," she called, "do you need help with the tray?"

She escaped into the kitchen, and when they returned, I was relieved that she had not mentioned my asking. As the widow had warned, Cullen Baker was a well-kept secret. People who knew him weren't going to admit it. I tried to get at the reason through Mack when we were alone. "Why does everyone seem afraid of Cully?"

He squirmed, scratching his neck, looking at his broken shoe. "I don' know."

"Of course you do. I won't tell Mrs. Loring that you told me."

He picked at the shell of a chestnut as if he didn't hear. I cast about for something to entice him but had nothing to give. "Cully is my friend. If people don't like him, I want to know why." I drew a deep breath and ventured, "Is it because he's cruel to his wife?"

His eyes swung round to me. "Mis' Cully a outlaw. Folk afraid he might shoot 'em."

"Mrs. Loring said he mistreats his wife. Does he?"

He shrugged one shoulder. "I don' know."

I'd get no more out of him, either. Someone—the widow or Cully—had coached him, for fear that wrong ears, likely soldier ears, might use information against Cully. For a while, I entertained the idea that the man I loved might be a spy. Civilians stole battle plans, carried contraband for surgeons. If that was his secret, I could understand why everyone was careful not to speak of him.

The only way I was going to learn the truth was to ask Cully.

Sometimes, to relieve the tiresome waiting, I went into town by myself—never staying long, in case he came while I was out of the house. Once when I entered the kitchen, Mack sat with a towel draped around his neck, and Mrs. Loring was wielding a large pair of scissors. She spoke without turning to me.

"You could do with a haircut, too, young man. Go wash your head, and I'll give you a clip."

My hands flew to my slowly growing curls and I took a couple of steps backwards. "No! I mean— You don't need to bother."

"No bother. Only take a few minutes."

"I'd—rather not, thank you anyway. Mother liked it long." The lame excuses piled one on another, until I faltered into silence and she just stared at me.

"Hmmmph. Well, if you want to look like a girl, it don't matter to me."

Trembling with mingled relief and aftermath of my fright, I cried silently, *Cully, hurry!* Sooner or later, my hair would grow to the point where she might not take *no* for an answer.

As October ended, I had more or less adjusted to the routine at Mrs. Loring's. Sometimes I was convinced that she knew Cully's whereabouts, yet I wasn't clever enough to pry the information from her.

I found myself thinking of him every moment, dreaming of him every night.

My mind warned me that, if he were indeed married, I was on a perilous course. But my heart wouldn't listen. I rehearsed what I would say to him face to face. Brought up to behave in a ladylike manner, I wasn't prepared to come right out and ask whether he had a wife, and, if he did, why he'd never told me about her but let me think he wanted me with him.

I decided that, since he'd admitted being afraid for me because living with him posed too many dangers, his leaving me here only proved how much he cared. He would clear away all my misgivings, without my having to question him.

94

From that moment on the porch when our eyes met in a jolt of mutual attraction, we'd known our fates were knotted. When he came back, we'd ride away, laughing over the jokes we'd pulled on Mrs. Loring, to the home he would make for me, and we would love each other for the rest of our lives.

By the middle of November only the oaks had not shed, and though mostly shriveled, the honeysuckle growing on the fence seemed as thick as ever. Leaves littered both yards, and I spent several days helping Mack with the heavy rake.

"We have to clean them up before it rains," Mrs. Loring told us. "If it once rains on a yardful of leaves, we'll have a real mess."

Wearing one of Mr. Loring's woolen shirts instead of my bulky coat, I worked up a sweat and an appetite. As I paused for breath, and to wipe a strand of hair out of my eyes, I watched Mack carry a tow sack to the bottom of the hill and dump its contents over the vine-ridden pasture fence that separated Mrs. Loring's property from the woods.

Beyond the fence, down the hill and screened by blackberry brambles, was the spring house. Mrs. Loring had stopped using it years ago, as she said the effort to make trips to it taxed her.

"I used to worry about some thief stealing my butter. I'd sit up here with my knee wrapped in hot towels, not feeling like moving, and think about how that churning wore me out, and just picture somebody making off with five pounds of butter or a gallon of milk, and I'd be sick. So I said to myself, I'll sell that cow and trade my preserves for butter and milk whenever I want it, and not worry about keeping anything down there."

Thinking now about butter and preserves made my mouth water. I drew in breath to call to Mack, who was dragging his feet and the tow sack. But Mrs. Loring stood on the porch. "Jess! Come here. I need to talk to you."

She was carrying my coat. "What is it?" I started forward, suddenly apprehensive. Behind me I could hear Mack panting as he caught up to me.

"Finish the raking," she ordered him, "and you can have hot cider."

To me, she said, "Let's go inside."

The kitchen was stifling after my exertion. I peeled off the outer shirt, careful to keep my back to the widow, but she laid hands on my shoulders and made me face her. After examining me, eyes boring into mine, she asked, "Does Cully know?"

"Know what?" I tried to appear innocent, but felt guilty through and through.

From behind her, she produced my envelope. "Don't think you can fool me any longer, Jessica Linville. I found this down in the lining of your coat. Now you tell me how you came to be with Cully."

I stared at the sealed envelope which I thought I'd lost long ago. In the lining, the whole time. Joshua had said, "You ever get in trouble, remember you got it." What did it contain? Not money, but something important.

"Give it to me," I said, with as much dignity as I could. "You had no right to open my letter."

"You can have it—I've no use for it—once you've told me what I want to know." She pulled up one of the chairs and sat, prepared to wait until I acquiesced.

"It happened the way I already told you. There was a brawl at the ferry and Cully let me join him. He was afraid if I stayed there, I'd get hurt."

"Does he know you're a girl?" she persisted.

"I never told him," I answered firmly. At least that was not among my lies.

She stared at me for several seconds, then said, "And just how does the only daughter of a plantation owner get herself mixed up in a brawl?"

The whole horrible episode crashed in on me, and I began to cry.

Mrs. Loring remained motionless, waiting for an explanation. Many were the nights she had read aloud the Scriptures concerning wickedness, and I was sure she would consider me wicked for deceiving her.

So, hard as it was, I told the old lady about the night Yankees burned my home, the death of Joshua, and my rescue by Cully at the landing. It was the best I could do without involving him in the deception.

"How long had you been with him?" she asked, and I couldn't tell from her tone what she thought.

At that moment, Mack came in, chanting, "Hot cider, hot cider, hot cider!" and I was reprieved until she had freshened the fire and put on the pot. She sent him out for stove wood and motioned me to continue.

"Only a few days," I told her, as I couldn't admit the truth.

"He make you sleep out on the ground?"

"A couple of nights we shared somebody's tent, but sometimes we stayed in a livery stable, and then in a barn."

She gave her customary short exhalation through her nose: "Hhummph!" Thoughtful, she got up to stir the cider, and the soft scrape of the wooden spoon across the bottom of the pot sounded loud in the silence. "What do you plan to do in the future?"

"I—I don't know." I certainly couldn't confide to her my dreams of marrying him. "You won't make me leave, will you?" The idea struck me cold with fear, as

I had no place to go, and if I did go, I would have to give up Cully.

"You never looked in this?" She held up my envelope, forgotten again in the confusion of trying to satisfy her curiosity.

"No. What's in there?" Whatever it was, I needed it now, for I was in about as much trouble as I could handle.

"One's a deed, made out to you. And a letter written by your father to his lawyer in San Francisco, asking help in securing valuable property there. Your grandfather's town house, left to you in his will."

I was not surprised. Papa had never failed in doing everything necessary to make my life pleasant. I said as much.

"Then I guess you'll be wanting to go out there and take possession of your inheritance."

"Well, yes, but—"

"If you need traveling money, there's plenty left from what Cully gave me."

"Thank you," I said, supposing I had better get it while she was feeling generous.

Mack staggered in with an armload of split wood and dropped it into the box. "Hot cider!" he beamed, and I was ready for it.

The document in the envelope and a promise of money gave me a security I had not experienced since the first year of the war, when we still thought the South would win. Now, having little hope of that, I wondered what kind of world Cully and I would be facing when the fighting did end.

"Well," the old lady said, "we'll talk more about it in the morning."

I was sure we would.

The next morning she asked, "Do you want me to go to the stage office with you and see if anything is running? San Francisco is a long way off, and there'll be a number of connections you'll have to make before you come to a rail line."

Trying to sound reasonable, I said, "Travel right now could be too dangerous. Perhaps I'd best wait until the war is over."

"Over! Lord, I don't think it'll ever be over." She pushed aside her half-eaten bowl of mush and stood up. "Well." She started to clear the breakfast dishes. "You think about it. If I had an inheritance waiting, I'd be in a hurry to claim it."

I was in no hurry. Just knowing the deed was safe in my repaired coat pocket gave me such confidence that I sang all the popular tunes I could think of while I scrubbed the porches. Now I had something to offer Cully besides my inexperienced self.

Under no illusions as to my abilities, I determined that whatever Mrs. Loring could teach me about homemaking, I would learn. Cully would teach me the rest.

Chapter Thirteen

One evening that same week, our supper of field peas and turnips was interrupted by an unexpected knock at the front door. Impatient, like the caller was a man, probably a soldier.

Mrs. Loring went to answer the summons, thinking Mack might not be able to handle the situation. Yankees were in the area, and she slept with Mr. Loring's horse pistol under her pillow at night.

Cully's voice, roughened by urgency, brought me up from my chair. He came through the dark hall, saying, "Whatever you can pack in a few minutes. It's all the time I've got. Jess, get your coat."

Gladly I snatched it off the peg. His beard had grown in and he was travel-stained and tense, on the run but in command.

"Mack, bring Apple's feed," he ordered, and to the widow, who was handing him a bundle, he said, "I won't forget this."

We went out to the back yard, where Mack met us with the horse. The chill, dim light of dusk made me wish we were staying at Mrs. Loring's. Hard as her shuck mattress was, I'd become spoiled, sleeping in a bed. But I was thrilled to be caught up in the middle of another adventure. I had known he wouldn't leave me here!

Attempting to mount, Cully dropped the bag of food. Startled, I bent to pick it up.

With a groan, he made it into the saddle. "Hurry, Jess." He reached down and we grasped each other's wrists, but he didn't seem able to hoist me up behind him.

Suddenly frightened, my fingers went numb and I let go. "Cully, what's the matter?"

He slumped onto Apple's neck. "Shot," he gasped. "They shot me."

Mack's shriek caused the horse to toss its head and sidestep, spilling Cully out of the saddle. I was knocked down trying to cushion his fall, but managed to keep his face from hitting the ground. Behind me, I heard Mrs. Loring coming, her words jabbing through my panic: "Oh, dear Lord! Oh, dear Lord!"

Sliding her arms under his shoulders, she lifted him to a sitting position, instructing, "Get him back on, quick."

"He can't ride!"

"He has to. If they find him in the house, we'll all hang. Help me!"

With Mack trying to soothe the horse, Mrs. Loring and I strained to lift Cully onto its back. He was barely conscious and gave little help or resistance.

"Where are we going?" I demanded, running alongside to prevent his falling again. On his other side, Mrs. Loring panted, "Spring house!"

Across the field we went, briars and dead weed stalks scraping us to the waist, and I was thankful for the trousers, which I had not discarded because of Mack. When we reached the fence Apple stopped, and I asked, "How do we get through?"

"Bars under the vines. Help me pull the top one out."

Thrusting my hands into the tangle, I gripped the splintery wood and cried, "Now!" We heaved with all our might—but the rail didn't budge. "It must be nailed!"

"No," she told me. "Try again."

Once, twice more we heaved. Then the honeysuckle gave up its hold and the bar slid loose. Dropping it, we persuaded Apple to jump the obstruction. Mack was dragged some in the process, but he sprang up, declaring, "I ain't hurt!"

We were making a great deal of noise, crashing through the huge piles of leaves Mack had dumped across the fence a few days earlier, and I glanced back, expecting riders to appear at any moment to give chase.

We left Mrs. Loring behind as the excited horse slid to the bottom of the hill with Mack and me straining to keep our feet from under the hooves, trying not to let Cully tumble off. He clung to the mane, unable to direct us or the animal. "Where is it?" I asked, breathless, seeing only a thick tangle ahead.

"Down in theah." Mack pointed into the mound of blackberry canes.

"How do we get to it?"

"Round heah."

Approaching from the other side proved possible even though rampant blackberry thorns and saw briars made it evident no one had been here for many seasons, and our clothing suffered. Our feet sank in damp ground, and I wished we had a light, to make sure no snake or other animal inhabited the place. "It's too small for Apple," I said. "We have to take him off and carry him inside."

I braced myself to receive Cully's weight. No longer conscious, he slid from the saddle like a grain sack—like Joshua. My heart seemed to ricochet in my chest. My prayer was a single cry: "Oh, God!"

"Listen!" Mack hissed, and besides Apple's snorts and the thud of shod hooves in mud, we could hear more hooves on the road, and men's voices shouting to each other.

"Hallo, there in the house!" one cried. "Come out. We are Russell's Arkansas Volunteers, and we mean you no harm."

I recognized that voice. Cully had predicted a time when he would be sorry for not killing the man who now chased him. I was sorry too. What would happen if the old lady resisted?

Through the underbrush and trees, we could see the glow of torches held aloft by searchers. There must have been half a dozen, some checking other houses up the street, a couple entering Mrs. Loring's home, one of them investigating an abandoned chicken coop at the edge of the yard.

"Get his feet," I commanded Mack. The limp body was difficult to manage, but we finally dragged Cully inside the springhouse.

Mack crouched beside me. "He dead?"

I searched for a pulse beat with trembling hands. "Not yet," I answered, and drew a long breath. "What about a doctor? Is there one in town?"

"Cain't get no doctor in town, but they's one out in the settlement."

"How far? Never mind—take the horse and go after him. If anybody stops you, make up a lie. Tell him Mrs. Loring fainted. Do whatever you have to, but for God's sake don't let on that Cully's here. And bring back that doctor!"

With no hesitation the child vanished on his mission, and I was alone with Cully.

Against the darkness my mind's eye saw Papa, Mama, Joshua, flames shooting against the night sky, the trashy men's gashed heads, Cap's body pinning me to the ground. Well, he hadn't forgotten the way I'd hit him nor being laughed at and tied up. He'd come after Cully with a vengeance.

I wondered what was happening up on the hill, for I could still hear distant voices calling to each other. Had they caught Mack? Were they questioning him, learning where Cully lay helpless? What would he do if strange men intercepted him, or if the doctor was away? Would he ride Apple into the yard, where the horse might be spotted by men left to watch the house?

A faint moan snapped my attention away from matters beyond my reach. "Cully?" I stroked his cheek. "Cully, it's all right—you're safe. Don't worry. Mack has gone for a doctor."

I didn't know if he heard me. My fingers fumbling at his unbuttoned coat, I was uncertain what I could do when I located the wound, beyond the idea of stanching a flow. My hands encountered an old bandage, stiff with dried blood, tied around him just below the ribs.

Unsure whether to be relieved or more worried, I moved to pillow his head on my lap. The beard flourished again untended, and beneath it the skin was hot. I pressed my fingertips to the pulse under his jaw. It beat steady, though his breathing was harsh and shallow and too quick.

Presently the raiders' voices came no more, and fog drifted over the field. I closed Cully's coat against the dampness and waited.

When my leg cramped, I shifted his position as gently as possible to the other. He stirred feebly, trying to sit up, mumbling. "Lie still," I pleaded, fearful he was delirious. I searched my pockets for the widow's handkerchief. Stretching, I could just reach the water bubbling among the rocks. As I wrung out the fabric and started to bathe his forehead, he muttered, "Mattie—? Mattie—"

Mattie—a nickname for Martha. My heart gave a flutter, like it did when I drank too much coffee. My mouth went dry. Using both hands, I cupped water and held it to my lips. He wouldn't have come for me if he didn't want me with him. If there was a Martha, he couldn't be married to her. I wouldn't believe it until I heard the words from him.

Outside, fog had turned to drizzle. Patter on the tin roof and on the ground beyond the door blended with the gurgle of running water. I was too cold to be sleepy, too tense to be lulled. Would Mack bring the doctor in time? or at all...

Having a lantern, or at least a candle, would have helped. Where was Mrs. Loring? What kept her from coming to us? I could picture her, stiff with disapproval, sitting with her hands folded in her lap while ruthless men lounged on her company sofa, waiting for Cully to turn up. Perhaps they had tied her wrists, and held a gun to her head.

I tried reviewing the plans I had made this last week, for Cully and the life we would have in San Francisco; but my mind would not remain on track. I chewed off a couple of fingernails, a habit I thought I'd beaten years ago. What would happen? Something must happen. Every night had to end. Even nightmares had an end.

Cully became restless again. He didn't try sitting up but moved his arms aimlessly, turning his head from side to side, muttering incoherently. I was afraid he might cry out, and did my best to soothe him with caresses and encouraging murmurs. If men were lurking, I didn't want them drawn by any noise.

Then he said clearly: "Locket... locket.... Must give it to Jess."

A thrill of hope and gratification ran through me. "I have it, Cully. The locket is safe. You're safe, too.

105

Everything's going to be all right." I spoke with certainty while inwardly chafing. Why didn't someone come? What was taking so long? I wished for a hot 'ginger tea' like Papa used to make for me when I was suffering from the grippe. One with plenty of whiskey, and a warm soft bed in which to sleep.

I stroked Cully's forehead, and he grew calm. Thick fog closed in the spring house doorway like a curtain, seeped into my clothing and made me shiver. I realized that the rain had stopped, and I'd been praying wordlessly for hours. In the deep silence and darkness, there was nothing I could do but pray and wait.

At least the searchers had not discovered us. Then Cully's breathing became rapid and I knew he was dreaming again. "Rest," I pleaded, afraid the wound would reopen. "Rest."

Clearly, so there was no mistaking, he said, "Mattie— I'll come home—this time—I swear—"

He broke off, groaning, but the damaging thing had been spoken. Home. To Mattie. To Martha. Before I could recover enough to cry, I heard hushed voices outside.

"Jess! Jess!" Mack's loud whisper called, as he fumbled his way to us. He had no light.

"We're here," I answered softly. "Careful you don't step on Cully."

He was gasping as though he'd run or walked a long way, and the bent figure with him wheezed like an elderly man. "What happened to the horse?" I asked. "Can't we have a lantern, or a candle? What can you do in the dark?"

"We don' do nothin' here, we take him up to the house. It safe now." The wheezy voice and competent hands that lifted Cully gave me confidence. "We lef' the hoss at my place, so nobody see him. We move Mist' Cully in the wheelbar."

The doctor held his shoulders, Mack his feet. I got up stiffly to trail behind them.

Taking the wheelbarrow up that hill was an ordeal I cringe to recall, though someone had had the foresight to cushion Cully's ride with a quilt. We tore out the rest of the fence, ripping our skin on splinters, exhausting our last reserve to carry him up the steps and into Mrs. Loring's dark kitchen.

She was ready for us, unshrouding a lamp and leading the way to her bedroom. All the windows had been covered to conceal our movements. She handed me the lamp. My arms trembled under its weight.

Helping to lay Cully on the bed, she sent Mack for a pair of Mr. Loring's wool socks. A great dark splotch covered his left side, below the ribs but above the hipbone. The doctor began tearing off the shirt.

"Jess, there's hot water on the stove. Go get it."

When I brought the kettle and a basin, the widow advised, "You better not stay."

The doctor, now that I could see him, was an aged black man in a faded black suit. He threw off his coat and, opening a threadbare carpet bag, laid out bladed instruments. Cully moaned as he and the widow soaked loose the old bandage and clotted blood.

The room was warm, but I was cold. "Call me, if—if—" I wanted to say, *If he asks for me*— but couldn't.

Mrs. Loring nodded, thinking she understood what I was feeling. "Get some sleep," she told me. "You'll have to sit with him later."

The same hurt that devastated me when she first mentioned someone named Martha Foster now made me slink up the dark stair. Again I drew the nightshirt of a dead man around me like a lover's arms and lay in a stranger's bed, staring dry-eyed at nothing.

Only a pinpoint of hope remained: perhaps they were not married. She existed, and he knew her, had feelings toward her, maybe even intimacy. But so long as there was no commitment, no bond made legal by a document, I yet might win him.

If he lived.

Tears came, filling my head with congestion. Too occupied with suppressing them in the pillow, I failed to notice when the door opened.

A hand on my shoulder made me whirl up. Mrs. Loring in a nightgown, shawl thrown around her against the cold, holding the lantern. I'd forgotten about her, and stared stupidly. She was as astonished as I.

"Why, you're in love with him!"

Her tone stopped my tears—and nearly stopped my heart. As she had done before, she demanded, "Does Cully know? Have you been lying to me?"

I shook my head, unable to speak, afraid I'd sob.

She wavered. At last she said, brusque, "Well, you'd best not let him find out. Wouldn't do either of you any good. There's hot gruel on the stove if you need it."

She settled herself under the covers, and I slid out on the other side and felt about the shadowed floor for my clothes. Of course she needed sleep, and it was my turn to sit with Cully.

I picked up the lantern and left, trembling. I had to uncover the truth, and only one person knew.

Chapter Fourteen

If he were awake and able to talk, did I dare ask? Postponing the answer, I went into the kitchen and dished up a portion of gruel. Mack came sleepily out of his cubbyhole, still dressed except for his feet.

"Are you hungry?" I was only making conversation, for he was always hungry. We stood near the stove, drawing its warmth and spooning in the food. There was little comfort in either. "What did the doctor say?"

"He say Mist' Cully mighty nigh died, but if'n he take his medicine he be all right in a few weeks."

A few weeks would give us opportunity to talk about my inheritance and what it might mean to our future. If Martha Foster had no permanent tie on him, I meant to pursue my plans. Placing my bowl on the table, I told Mack, "Hurry and finish so I can take the light with me." He obediently downed the last bites.

Eagerness and dread mingled as I opened Mrs. Loring's bedroom door. A lamp turned low already shed enough light that I could see objects in the room: dresser with a framed mirror, washstand with basin and pitcher, clean towels, a heavily-draped window facing the road, and a wardrobe with hatboxes piled on top. On the last wall, beside the door, was the bed upon which they had lain Cully. He was awake. I hadn't expected that.

"Hello," I said, and cleared my throat. "Shall I blow out this light?"

"I don't need it," he said, faintly. His eyes closed.

I extinguished the lantern flame and sat on the chair beside him with my feet on the rung and my hands clasped in my lap. After a long minute, eyes still shut, he asked, "How do you like Mrs. Loring?"

"Well enough." I wanted to say more, but couldn't get my thoughts sorted before he continued: "She hasn't—" He drew a short breath as if doing so hurt him. "found out you're a girl?"

"I want to talk to you about that. When you're better." Stalling, I wet my lips. "How do you feel?"

"Bad," he admitted. "Bandage is too tight, and that damned medicine makes me sick."

"The doctor said—"

"I know what he said." He coughed gently. "Guess I gave you all a scare, didn't I."

"Yes. Do you think those men will return?"

"Don't worry, I'll be gone when they do."

"Where will you go?" My heart thudded with possibility. No one would chase him all the way to San Francisco, not even Cap. He would be safe with me.

"Line Ferry, until I can ride again."

The thudding stopped, suspended, like my breathing. At last I got the question past clenched teeth: "What's there?"

"That's where I live. When I'm not dodging damned Yankees and turncoats."

I cleared my throat a couple of times. "Tell me about Line Ferry. If you feel like talking."

"Not much to tell." His eyelids closed. "Got folks there."

My head suddenly felt giddy. I wanted him to go on, yet dreaded what he would say. When I'd asked him about family, he'd told me he didn't know—or care—where they were. "Your parents?"

"No. I guess they're probably dead."

I had to ask. "Who, then?"

For a long moment I thought he wouldn't answer, but at last the reply came, soft and muffled. "Martha—and some in-laws."

Clutching the edges of the chair, I sat motionless until the dizziness subsided. By that time Cully had fallen asleep. I could tell by the way his cheek pressed against the pillow.

When I was sure I could move without breaking into hundreds of pieces like the shards of a dropped mirror, I picked up a water glass from the night stand and drank. Then I bathed my hot face with a corner of a towel dipped in the basin.

Going to the window, I peeked between the closed drapes. Morning, gray as it was, still advanced. The rest of the world hadn't come to an end. There were even a few people on the street.

Mrs. Loring tiptoed in, bearing a tray with fresh oatmeal and a cup of steaming coffee. Seeing that he was resting, she whispered, "Go ahead and eat this. You look like you can use it."

I accepted the coffee. "Thank you." The sight of oatmeal nauseated me, but a cup gave me something to hold on to.

"You should eat," the old lady said. "Coffee by itself like that can turn on you."

"Maybe later." We stood near each other in the center of the room, she holding the tray, I sipping my coffee, both looking at Cully.

"He'll be fine in a week or two," she reminded me.

"Mack told me."

"Let's go in the other room."

I followed her to the parlor, knowing what she would say. She didn't waste any time saying it. "You can't keep riding around with him, feeling like you do. Once he suspects—" Her lips thinned into a tight line before she continued, "He's not the sort of gentleman you are probably used to. If your mother were alive—"

"Don't!" My voice trembled. What would she think if I told her he'd known all along that I was no boy? Now I understood why he had insisted that I go on pretending. 'How would it look,' he'd said that first evening, 'me riding around with a gal on my saddlebags? I got a reputation to think about.' And a wife, living in Line Ferry.

"Will you go on to San Francisco," she persisted, "and leave Cully alone?"

Coming between a man and his wife, even if I were capable of doing so, was not something for which I wanted to take responsibility. At last I gave a sigh of defeat. "I will go to San Francisco. But I want to say good-bye."

"There'll be time for that. Get your coat, and let's see if anybody's at the stage office."

When the route was mapped out and my ticket paid for, I let Mrs. Loring go in to spell Mack. The child came out to the kitchen, where I was warming my hands at the stove, trying to overcome my misery.

"Mist' Cully axin' for you."

My heart began racing. Had Mrs. Loring told him I was leaving? Would he try to stop me? If he did, could I keep my word?

I met her in the doorway. "Mack says Cully wants to see me."

"Be careful what you say," she warned.

I hurried along the dim hall, so tense and excited that my head ached. Closing the door behind me, I stood with my hands on the knob and tried to read his mood.

He was propped on two large pillows, covered to the middle of his chest. Though the front of his flannel shirt hung open, I couldn't see the bandage which I knew hid beneath the faded counterpane. I stood rigid with uncertainty.

"Jess," he said, patting the edge of the bed, "sit here and talk to me."

I crept forward and eased myself down, out of reach. Dark and drowsy from the medicine, those eyes charmed me. "What shall I talk about?"

"Is it raining?"

"Drizzly. Are you cold? I can get another blanket."

"No, just wondered. Mrs. Loring won't open the curtains. I hate being closed in."

"She's afraid."

"Are you afraid?"

"A little. Aren't you?"

He slid his hand under the pillows and brought out his pistol. "Not with this close by. Rascals ambushed me. Too cowardly to stand up and fight."

He grimaced, and I asked, "Can I do anything to make you more comfortable?"

His rare smile wrenched my heart. "You could get me a pint of whiskey."

My own smile was shaky. "Mrs. Loring wouldn't approve."

"You like her?"

"She's been good to me."

"Think you'd like to stay with her?"

Biting my lip and looking at my hands clasped in my lap, I tried to speak, cleared my throat, and at last said, "My father arranged a place for me to go. San Francisco. I have a deed to some property there. He would want me to take charge of it."

Cully looked at me with mild wonder, but all he said was, "Well, hell, Jess, I thought you were penniless, and here you are a landowner."

Disappointment filled me. I realized that, no matter how pride and honor suffered, no matter what promises I had made, I wanted him to persuade me to change my mind. After all, he would be in Line Ferry, far enough away from Mrs. Loring's house that my presence could do no harm. Sometimes I might see him when he was in town, but I wouldn't reveal how I felt.

"I—I'll miss you." I needed to hear him say he would miss me, or give a sign that the crossing of our lives meant something to him.

"When are you leaving?"

He sounded concerned, and I watched for any reaction that would reveal deeper emotion. "As soon as the stage to Fort Worth has enough passengers to make the run."

With a laugh, he said, "That might be awhile."

"I don't mind." Before I could stop them, bitter words sprang out. "Why didn't you tell me about Martha? Remember, when I asked, you said you didn't have a home!"

We stared at each other, and through a blur of tears, I saw his expression mellow. He held out one hand to me. "Come here, Jess."

I wanted to go to him—but I didn't dare. Being in the same room with him provoked a kind of pain I had never before experienced, a yearning I only partly understood.

"Come here," he repeated. His eyes held an expression I couldn't fathom.

Moving to sit beside him, I let him take my hand. This near, his fingers warming mine, I longed to hear him say that he loved me, and I would have done anything to have him hold me close and promise to stay with me forever. But he was silent, looking down.

"At first," he said slowly, "I thought you were just a kid, and there was no reason to tell you. Later on, when I found out different, it was too late."

"But you came back," I whispered. "Why?"

He looked up then. "Don't you know?"

"Tell me."

114

Soft, he said, "I was afraid I'd die without seeing you again."

Tears streamed off my chin. "Cullen Baker afraid? I don't believe it."

His thumb caressed my skin, smearing the wet streaks. His fingertips along my jawline urged me toward him. Leaning, I watched his lips part slightly. I shut my eyes, causing my mouth to land a little to one side; but he made the adjustment. He must have sensed my need, for he didn't hold back. His mouth tasted of ginger and wild cherry, and my heart shook me with its uneven beat. This was the kind of caress he gave his wife.

After a bit, I reluctantly let him end the only kiss I'd ever have from him. Yet we remained so close that his mustache brushed against my lips when he said, with tender warning, "Take care, Jess."

Dazed, I answered, low and fierce, "I don't care! I love you, Cully. Kiss me like that again."

"Ah, Jess." His hands smoothed my hair, cradled my head. "You don't know what you're asking."

It was all I could do not to throw myself on his chest and beg him to go with me. Only his wound—and the threat of dishonor—kept me in check.

Into the silence that stretched between us, he asked, "Got money for a ticket?"

I nodded, cheeks hot from passion and anger at the injustice of life.

He lay against the pillows and sighed. "Guess I never should have picked you up in Dorn's Landing."

"I'm not sorry about that," I declared. "Are you?"

Pondering a moment, he decided. "No. You made me mad as hell a couple of times, but you're pretty good company."

When I came out of Cully's room, the taste of his kisses still vivid and the agony of loss making me tremble, the old lady told me, "I've been to the Harrisons' place. They're ready to move west, and there's five of them, so if you go with them, old McFee won't have any excuse not to send out a stage."

"You know I don't want to do this."

"You don't have any choice."

Yes, I do, I thought. *I could make him run away with me.* But I didn't argue.

Cully and I didn't see each other again until he came into the kitchen the morning of my departure.

The widow was packing a lunch for me in a basket, but when he appeared in the doorway she left the task with a muttered excuse. She'd sent Mack to stay with a neighbor, as I was wearing one of her dresses, taken in to fit me, and carried a bonnet and an old purse. "I'd never be able to explain if he saw you like that," she'd told me.

"You leaving already?" Cully gripped the door jamb to steady himself.

"I have to." I finished tying the twine on my lunch.

"Then we'd better say goodbye here. I don't care to show my face on the street until I know who my friends are."

I crossed the room and hugged him, loosely because of the wound, my cheek against his coarse cotton shirt. It smelled fresh from drying on the line.

"Your hair's growing out," he noted, running his fingers through its thickness. "And you look different in a dress."

"Cully—" I drew away enough to see him. "I meant what I said, about lov—"

His hand came lightly over my mouth. "No, Jess. It's all best forgotten."

"Oh, don't say that! I don't want to forget, and I don't want you to."

116

"You'll change your mind." He smiled a little, though the expression in his eyes was far from happy. "Look, Jess, I don't know what you expected, but if things could go on the way they were, I'd not object. Only, they can't. You know why."

"I know. I just hoped—"

"Don't hope. I've done a lot of things people think are wrong, but I can't change this."

I could hear the widow's heels striding along the upstairs hall. Any moment, she would be descending to accompany me to the stage. I tiptoed, he bent his head, and I kissed his bearded cheek. Tears blinding me, I heard him say, "Ah, hell, Jess—" and he gathered me in his arms.

We were still locked in that embrace when the old lady's voice broke in. "Best leave now, if you mean to catch the stage."

Cully didn't acknowledge her. He kissed me, slow and hard, as if imprinting the feel of our yearning lips for all those days ahead. Then he drew away, eyes holding mine. "I won't forget."

Chapter Fifteen

San Francisco in 1864 was as different from East Texas as life there had differed from my childhood.

A seaport, it rivaled New Orleans in established buildings and busy streets. My first action was to find Grandfather's lawyer, a Mr. Mills.

His office was dark, having only one large window and dim gas lights. It was furnished with a walnut desk, shelves, and chairs. The carpet was worn, but the room was tidy, and he was genial.

"Everything appears to be in order," he said, stuffing my few papers into the envelope. "Of course, the house hasn't been used for years and will have to be reopened. Until we can locate a suitable guardian, it will be best for you to stay with my wife and me. You must be exhausted after such a long journey."

Too exhausted to resist having to live in another strange place, or object to his appointing a guardian for whom I felt no need. I nodded and went with him.

For three weeks I remained at Mr. Mills' home, doing light housework for my room and board, as there was no cash money in the will, only the house and a stipend for its upkeep. His wife spoke softly and sometimes sang hymns that I supposed were meant to soothe my troubled spirit.

Christmas came and went, festive with the Mills' children and grandchildren visiting. They decorated a tree with popcorn and paper chains of snowflakes and fragile glass balls.

Did Mrs. Loring bring in a tree for Mack? Was Cully in Line Ferry, visiting his wife, exchanging gifts? Somehow, I couldn't picture that. 'I hate being closed in,' he'd told me. 'She stays home,' Mrs. Loring had once said of Martha.

What an odd sort of marriage, I thought. She needed someone to stay home with her, and he needed someone who thrived in the open air, scorning the comforts of feather beds for the harsh life of camp and trail.

After the holiday, Mr. and Mrs. Mills and I went to inspect the house. Workmen had repaired steps and shingles, re-paned windows that had suffered the thoughtlessness of vandals, and cleared debris from the yards. Two stories of deep red brick, a moss green roof, and wood lattices painted white, gave the place an inviting atmosphere. Two large trees had long ago been planted at either side of the gravel walk. I wondered what color their leaves would turn next fall.

As I stepped onto the wide front porch, my breath caught in my throat. A chair was pulled up near the railing and sat a little askew, as though someone had been sitting there, watching the street, and had just left.

I must have faltered or grown pale, for Mrs. Mills leaned toward me, brow furrowed. "Child, are you all right?"

"Yes, thank you," I answered her. But I made a point of asking Mr. Mills to have the workmen remove that chair the next day.

I was not disappointed in the house. The upstairs had a separate entrance, and eight rooms enabled me to take boarders. At first Mrs. Mills tried to dissuade me, but in a matter of days a young couple was settled, and I deposited their first month's rent into my new bank account.

My own living quarters were quite comfortable. I chose a bedroom located at the back of the house away from the noisy street, with a sitting room connected. Aunt Sis slept in a large room next to the kitchen.

A front parlor for receiving guests made me feel capable and independent. Clothing which Mrs. Mills gave me, two new bonnets, high-heeled boots, and last year's parasol added to my sense of respectability; though as soon as I had money, I took Aunt Sis shopping and replaced everything with items of my choice. For those first weeks, I was too busy during the day to think of Cully.

But when the nights came, I missed the chill of sleeping on the ground near him, the whispers of animals stealthing through the underbrush, the aroma of smoke from campfires and coffee heating in a tin can. I missed the excitement of galloping along rutted dirt roads or whipping between low-branched trees in the thickets of East Texas, Apple's hard-muscled legs pounding through the swamp mud—and Cully's equally hard-muscled legs outlined against mine, his arms circling me when I rode in front.

I even missed Mrs. Loring swiping at the errant strands escaping her hair pins, her brusque manner, her tireless chatter. Several times I caught myself starting to call Mack to bring in stove wood, or expecting him to pop up and beg me to play a game of draughts.

While I yearned for the cold drizzle of East Texas instead of the fogs and mists of this unfamiliar country, one thing was fortunate. Aunt Sis was an accomplished cook, so I was well-fed. When I described the flavors of the dish Mrs. Loring called "Aunt Annie's East Texas Cornbread," she experimented a day or so with cornmeal, tomato sauce, white beans, onions, and hot peppers, and brought the result to me for approval.

"Perfect!" I declared, tears in my eyes.

"You shuah it's not too hot?"

"It's just right," I assured her, proving it by eating three helpings.

It was no accident that I met Ed that first month. He was Mr. Mills' nephew who lived across town and frequently helped his uncle with legal matters, such as evictions, wording notices appearing in newspapers— and finding lost or runaway people. "Like a detective," I remarked.

His aunt placed him opposite me at the dinner table, giving us no choice but to look at each other over the roast beef and vegetables.

The word startled him, but he seemed pleased to think of himself that way. "Somewhat like one, I suppose. I keep a record of bits of information, clues if you like, and fit the pieces of the puzzle together. If I'm lucky."

"He's always lucky," Mr. Mills stated with pride. "But that's because he makes his luck. Don't you, Ed? Handsome, too, just like his uncle."

Ed *was* handsome, in a clean, trimmed sort of way. His blue eyes were wide and frank, his face boyishly in want of a beard, and his light brown hair thick and fine and soft as a woman's. His teeth had never known the taint of tobacco, and his hands had never held a gun.

Guileless enough, in fact, so that he suspected no under-handedness on my part when I made a request a few days later in my parlor, where I had invited him to tea.

"I want you to find someone for me." I poured from the ceramic pot as casually as though my heart was not speeding. "I used to keep track of him through a friend, but she has stopped answering my letters."

Truthfully, Mrs. Loring hadn't answered any of the three I had sent at points along my journey, with

121

instructions to reply to me at Mr. Mills' address. I understood why she wouldn't, but her refusal to give me news about Cully made me determined to have it.

"I'll try," Ed agreed. "Tell me all you can about the person." He took out his little notebook.

What could I tell? Not why I needed the services of an investigator, nor that Cully was the leader of outlaws who recognized neither side in the war but stole from whoever had more than they did in order to give to their friends. Not that I had once entertained the idea he might be a spy, for I no longer believed that. Certainly not that I'd ever ridden with him, slept in the same blanket, kissed his lips. Not that I loved him.

"His name is Cullen Baker, and he should be somewhere in the vicinity of—" My voice broke, and I tried to hide the fact with a cough and a sip of tea. "Line Ferry, in East Texas. If he isn't there, he might be in Dorn's Landing. He—" I cleared my throat.

I watched Ed jotting down the information. "His—wife's name is Martha. She was a Foster. He has—curly hair—medium brown, and he wears it long. His eyes are the color of..." My thoughts returned to the day on the porch.

"The color of—?" Ed prompted me.

I gave a laugh that sounded cynical to my own ears. "The swamp pools at sunset."

He laughed, too, softly, in surprise. "That isn't very flattering."

"Have you ever seen an East Texas swamp, Ed?" I smiled.

"Not that I remember. I take it, you have."

"Yes. It has its own beauty."

Neither of us spoke for a minute, until he resumed writing. "Approximate age? Height?"

"About like you, maybe a little—" How to explain, without offending? Tougher. Leaner. More—alluring.

"What sort of work does he do?" Ed asked, seeing that I couldn't finish. I was still at a loss with this question. He rescued me. "Well, this will give me a start. Now, what do you want to know about him?"

"He—" I had to swallow to keep my voice steady. "He was wounded a few weeks ago. I just want to know that he is all right. And anything else in the way of news."

"I'll do my best," Ed promised.

Ten days later he came to my door with his report. His first words were, "Jessie, how well do you know this man?"

As we took seats on my horsehair sofa, I kept my eyes averted. "Why, not very well, actually. Why?"

"He seems to have made himself a reputation for being ruthless. One source calls him an outlaw. While he hasn't come to trial for his activities, several incidents involved shooting people." His honest face was troubled. "Killing them."

"That happens, in a war," I pointed out. "Where is he now?"

He flipped a page of his notebook. "He tends to disappear for weeks at a time. My contact traced him to the home of a Mrs. Loring, but he left there before Christmas. Nothing could entice her to reveal where he had gone, though my contact said he was sure she knew."

"Was—was he recovered? Did your man question Martha Foster?"

"Oh, yes, she is living in Line Ferry, as you thought. But that is in Perry County, Arkansas, and not Texas. No matter. She claimed she hadn't seen Baker in more than a month. As for his health, you mustn't worry. We finally located the doctor who treated his wound, and it was not serious."

Giving a short sigh, I said, "Well, thank you for all the effort. Please tell me your fee, and I will make out a bank draft."

Ed pocketed the notebook and picked up his hat. Instead of putting it on, he stood nervously twirling it by the brim between his hands. "I'd like for you to have dinner with me, Jessie. Will you?"

The abruptness of his invitation threw me into confusion. We often ate at his uncle's home, but this was different. He was asking me out, to a restaurant.

Striving to accept graciously, I answered, "I am honored."

"I'll bring a carriage around at six." He sounded a bit breathless. "If that's all right."

"Yes." We moved toward the door. He squeezed my hand for a moment before turning to leave, whistling.

When he was gone, a thought struck me: should I ask Aunt Sis to accompany us as chaperone? Was it proper for a young lady my age to dine alone with a man, or would Ed be offended at the presence of a third party? I did not know. When I asked Aunt Sis, she just laughed. "Honey, you as safe with that boy as you are in a church."

"I don't doubt that," I answered. "But how will it look, just the two of us, out after dark?"

"Folk who know him won't think anything bad, and nobody else matter."

One of the reasons I liked Aunt Sis so much was her use of common sense, and I told her so.

The freedom of San Francisco was far from the wilds of East Texas, but less confining than the life I would have had on the bayou.

Nightmares still haunted me, so that sometimes I walked the halls of my plantation home, shared a candlelit dinner with Papa and Mama, lazed on the front balcony on a balmy spring morning, and dreamed that I woke to find myself in my old canopy bed at the top of the stairs, with all my childhood treasures. Sensing myself to be alone always jarred me from sleep.

However, this new life had its pleasures. Ed took me out frequently, to the exclusion of other young ladies. His aunt expressed her approval. "He's getting to the age that he ought to be thinking of settling down. You too."

The four of us played popular parlor games, or Ed and I would supper with the couple who boarded with me, or we spent pleasant evenings sitting in front of the fire, sipping tea or cocoa. Once Aunt Sis came in with a tray and a smile. "Hot cider!" she announced, "Hope you all like it."

Memories flooded my thoughts, but I managed to pretend interest in what Ed was saying so that he didn't notice my inner agitation.

When Lee surrendered, and most of the fighting stopped, I wondered whether Cully would go home to Martha as he'd vowed he'd do, that night in the spring house, when he was wounded and unaware of what he was saying.

I gave serious consideration to the property my family had owned on the bayou. Mr. Mills said he would look into matters for me and I left the details in his hands. New friends occupied much of my time, as well as concerts and lectures—usually with Ed, but sometimes with other eligible young men. I engaged in long conversations about politics and fashions, kept up with events and trends by reading newspapers and magazines, made the rounds of old book shops in order to build my library.

Gradually, worries about what Cully was doing faded, and dreams of him at night came no more. A year passed, leaving me with feelings of nostalgia whenever I remembered those days spent with him in the Sulphur River country.

One afternoon in spring, Ed came unexpectedly. He said, "I have another report, if you want to hear it."

I wasn't sure that I did. Already, my heart began speeding in the familiar, uncomfortable way, and my palms grew damp. Yet I had to know. "I was not aware you were still making inquiries."

His cheeks flushed slightly. "I was curious," he admitted. "I almost decided not to tell you."

"Why? Has something happened to him?"

Ed looked uneasy. "Not exactly." He took a deep breath and exhaled. "His wife died."

I could not immediately sort my reactions. Part of me was sorry, for Martha who had died, for Cully who probably loved her—in his own way. Yet a deeper, primordial part exulted. He was free!

Chapter Sixteen

Feverishly my brain gathered strands of half-formed intentions—in spite of my promise to Mrs. Loring and to myself. I realized that, all this time, I'd been immersing myself in many activities while planning, *scheming,* a reason to see Cully again. Now I could. There was nothing to stop me.

Some of what I was thinking clearly showed, for Ed reached out and took my hand, leaning toward me earnestly. "Jessie, there's more."

"What more?" Details sped through my mind: Aunt Sis could manage things here without me. My bank account was sufficient to make the trip—

"He dressed an effigy in Martha's clothing. For weeks he refused to leave the house or allow anyone to enter. At last he agreed to send the child to—"

"Child!" Ed had my attention now. "There was a child?"

"A daughter, about four years of age. She was the issue of a previous marriage, to—"

"Stop!" I gripped his arm. "Let me take in all this." I sat with closed eyes, realizing that all the while I was with Cully, he had not only a wife, but a child as well. 'By a previous marriage.' That morning when I tried to persuade him to leave the country and avoid Cap, he'd told me, "I got obligations here." Now, I knew what he'd meant.

I heard Aunt Sis ask, "Shall I bring hot coffee, sir?" and Ed answered, "Yes, I think we will need it."

The grandfather clock in the hallway ticked like an oversize heartbeat. In the kitchen, clinks of cups against saucers and both against a tray, marked Aunt Sis's movements.

Faint, I sipped the coffee she brought. At last I began to realize it didn't matter. That first, unknown woman who had married him and had a child with him must be dead, too. Otherwise, he could not have married Martha.

"What happened to her? The first wife?"

"Jane Petty. She died sometime in 1860. Baker also had difficulty adjusting to her death, for he drank heavily at the time and was unable to care for the child properly."

Ed wasn't lying. I knew that, knowing him. "Where is Cully now?"

"From all I can learn, he's hiding out in the swamps again."

The enormity of the task ahead was disheartening, though the end of the war and partially restored railroad linkage made the prospect more appealing.

"I know what you're thinking, Jessie," Ed said gently. "Please don't go through with it. I will keep track of him for you, if I can."

Ed was as good as his word, though information was scant and not always pleasant.

Many times during the next year, I almost made the grueling journey to the place I would find Cully. But, if the conflicting and garbled telegrams coming from Ed's contacts in Arkansas and Texas could be believed, one thing was clear: untamed as he was when I met him, now he had lost all tenderness. This knowledge grieved me, for I was convinced that the things happening to him were none of his fault.

"The governor of Texas would not put up a reward of one thousand dollars if he were innocent," Ed told me when I tried to defend him. "The man has terrorized half a dozen counties by shooting and beating people whenever he feels like it."

'Is there a reward out for you?' I'd asked Cully, and he'd answered, 'Not yet, but I reckon there will be one day.' Would I be of any use to him, appearing out of the past, or had he forgotten all about me? 'I won't forget,' he'd promised. I believed him. But it didn't mean he wanted me there.

"If you'd had soldiers and bushwhackers chasing you, you would probably shoot and beat people, too," I declared.

"The war's been over for two years, Jessie. You can't use it to excuse him any longer."

"The war won't be over for the South for another generation." I based my conviction on newspaper accounts of the devastated economy of my homeland. "I'd like to hear Cully's side in all this."

"Well, we won't argue about it." Ed walked to the door. "Shall I pick you up at the usual time?"

"I suppose so," I answered.

If Ed continued his investigation, he didn't tell me. And I didn't ask. Hearing him call Cully a murderer, a fugitive with a price on his head, wrenched my heart.

It hurt to admit there was nothing I could do to help. Mrs. Loring had never responded to my letters. She wasn't likely to welcome me on her doorstep, even if Cully was free of the marriage bond. He still had a child, and in-laws who might resent my intrusion. Gradually, I gave up immediate plans, though I clung to my dreams that someday, Cully and I would find each other again.

Though other men courted me, my friendship with Ed grew until I found myself caring about him. And he cared for me, for he asked me to marry him. As kindly as I could, I told him, "I'm not ready to marry anyone."

"Am I making a fool of myself, hoping you'll change your mind?"

"You could never make a fool of yourself, Ed."

The only thing that prevented a commitment was my attachment to the man who had rescued me from a mob in Dorn's Landing.

"Jessie," Ed greeted me one spring day in 1869, "I'm going to ask you once more, and I want you to give it thought before you answer. Will you marry me, or am I going to have to ask Mary Ellen Fulton?"

Mary Ellen was something of a joke between us, being an invention of Ed's, but I could tell that, after two proposals, his patience was thin and this would be my last opportunity to be Mrs. Edward Terry.

He joined me at a long table in front of a shed in the side yard, where I had set up pots, trowels, and small tubs of fertile dirt, and fancied myself a Sunday gardener. Today I was sorting bulbs I planned to arrange in a border along the front walk.

"Which do you like better, Ed, daffodils or tulips?" The bright slant of sunshine made me squint up at him.

Dressed for dinner at a new restaurant, he looked as clean as the wind-swept blue sky, and as uncomplicated. "I like violets," he said, taking one of my grubby hands and turning it palm up. "I suppose you gave the yard boy the day off."

"No," I replied in a lighthearted tone that matched his, "I dismissed him. He didn't know the difference between an azalea and a plum tree."

"Cruel Jessie! Now the poor lad has no wage to support his widowed mother."

"Oh, he'll never miss the pittance I paid him. And he'll have time to sit on the docks and watch the ships come in. Seriously, Ed, he would do better in a job that paid more. Why don't you ask Uncle James to find room for him at your office?"

"I might do that, if—"

"Miss Jessie!" Aunt Sis called to us as she hurried across the sloping lawn. "Miss Jessie, this letter come for you."

I couldn't imagine who might have sent me a letter, except my estranged aunt. When I decided to sell the bayou property, Mr. Mills had been in touch with her, in case she wanted to buy it; but she had not done so.

The envelope was addressed to me, in care of Mr. Mills. Unfamiliar handwriting conveyed nothing, but the postmark was Texas. Only two people in Texas knew of my connection with the lawyer. Shaking with excitement, I tore open the message and looked for the signature.

Only slightly disappointed to see that it was from Mrs. Loring, I turned to Ed. "Come up to the house and let's sit on the porch. Aunt Sis has made a pitcher of lemonade."

Tucking the letter under my arm, I walked beside him, glad I had not given a quick 'yes' to marriage. There must be news of Cully, or the old lady never would have written. Savoring the anticipation, I washed my hands and joined Ed, who was lounging on a cushioned wicker chair and sipping from a tall glass.

"Is it anything important?" he asked.

"I don't know yet." I unfolded the pages and glanced at them, searching for Cully's name. It came halfway down on the second sheet.

Cully was killed back in January.

For several moments, my eyes kept reading the same line, trying to make sense of it. Three months had passed, happy months during which I had felt no qualm, no premonition. I couldn't believe what she had written, but expected the message to change.

"Jessie, what's wrong?" I heard Ed say, his voice tense with concern. Though he was leaning toward me, I had no power to answer. I'd never fainted before, but this must be what it was like.

"Jessie, talk to me." He came around the table to kneel and peer into my face. "What's happened?"

I nudged the sheet toward him, thinking how different he and Cully were in so many ways—and how alike in one. With surprising detachment, I wondered what else Mrs. Loring had written, but I realized that mattered little now.

"Oh Lord," Ed murmured, reading, and a moment later his warm hands found mine. "I'm sorry, Jessie. I know you cared about him. Is there anything I can do?"

Drawing a painful breath, I told him, "Hold me."

As he put his arms around me, I heard the whisper of the stationery falling to the porch. Now, when Ed asked me to marry him, nothing stood in the way.

Epilogue

Maybe, if I'd gone back, like I wanted to— Well, I can't let myself worry about that. Ed Terry was good to me, and I was happy for a lot of years as his wife. But I never forgot those exciting days riding with

Cully through East Texas thickets, nor the adventures we'd shared.

In some other time and place, his life might have been different. I often think of all the bad things folks said about him, particularly a man named Thomas Orr, who wrote a dirty little book called *Life of the Notorious Desperado Cullen Baker, from His Childhood to His Death, with a Full Account of All the Murders He Committed.*

Ed wouldn't let me tell Mr. Orr what I thought of him when the book was published; said I ought to read it before making any judgements. But I always tell people now— Say what they might, nobody knew him the way I did. I rode with Cullen Baker.

The End

Aunt Annie's East Texas Cornbread

Sort and rinse 1 heaping cup dried navy beans, then soak overnight in enough water to cover by 1 inch.

Next day drain beans and place in a heavy bottom pot with water to cover by 2 inches. Over high heat, bring to a boil, skimming off the white foam that rises. Cover with a tight lid. Move to cooler spot and simmer for about 45-minutes to an hour.

While beans are still a bit firm, add 1 teaspoon of salt and stir, and leave the pot on the stove to soak up the salt. It is important not to add salt to dried beans until they are mostly cooked.

While the beans are cooking, put 2 slices of bacon or fatback in a large skillet over medium heat and slowly cook until the fat is rendered. (Do not let the bacon get too crisp.) Remove the bacon from the pan and lay on a paper-covered plate. When cool enough to handle, crumble or chop the bacon and set aside.

Finely chop ½ a large onion and some chile peppers. Cook in the skillet over medium heat till the onions are clear-ish, while you cut up 4-5 peeled and chopped medium-sized tomatoes. Save the juice in a small bowl.

Add tomatoes to the skillet. Continue cooking until quite thick (about 30 minutes), then stir together 2 teaspoons brown sugar, ½ teaspoon ground dried mustard, and a good pinch of cayenne, and add to the sauce.

Add the drained beans, the chopped bacon, and enough of the tomato juice and bean cooking liquid to cover. Simmer together for 15 minutes, adding additional liquid as necessary to cover. Keep hot.

Next heat up the oven while you make the cornbread topping. In a mixing bowl, whisk together ¾ cup corn meal, ¼ cup flour, 1 ½ teaspoons baking powder, and ¼ teaspoon salt.

Blend together ½ a beaten egg, 1 tablespoon olive oil , and ½ cup milk. Add to the cornmeal mixture and stir together. Let sit until thickened.

Coat a 1 ½ quart dish with butter before adding the hot bean mixture. Carefully lay spoonfuls of the thickened cornbread mix over the beans to cover everything. DO NOT press down, but gently smooth the top of the cornbread.

Note well: Keep the bean mixture soupy, as the cornbread dough will drink up much of the liquid. Let the cornbread batter thicken before you pour it over the beans. Other wise, it will sink down into the beans and everything runs together which is not what you want.

Bake for 25-35 minutes until the cornbread topping is nicely browned. Spoon out portions and serve while hot.

This dish goes nice with a mess of collard greens.

If you enjoyed
I Rode with Cullen Baker

additional copies may be purchased using links to a
secure shopping cart
via
www.rlbhartmann.com

You'll find book covers, videos, photo illustrations,
a character list, news, and Buy links on the website.
There you can also preview

the epic
Cordero Saga
TIERRA DEL ORO
A Novel in Nine Books

Forty Grains of Black Powder
Legend of the Sierra Madre
Los Pobres
La Puerta del Sol
A Lion Against the Wind
Bitter Victory
Tierra y Libertad
The Horse Tamers
Tesoro

One story, one family, one continuing adventure!

www.ingramcontent.com/pod-product-compliance
Lightning Source LLC
Chambersburg PA
CBHW072001170626
46813CB00005B/1968